The Truth About Elves

D1400226

EKTA R. GARG

atmosphere press

Published by Atmosphere Press

Cover design by Kevin Stone

Atmospherepress.com

Dedication:
To Mom and Dad
Thank you for teaching me
about the value of stories
and the magic in storytelling.
I love you.

Prerna rubbed her hands together as she hurried down the long hallway outside Mr. C's office. Glad to be out of the cold, she brushed a few snowflakes from her shoulders then unlocked the door to the waiting room and went inside. She flicked on the lights and moved to the desk to turn on the computer, then docked her iPod in the office music system.

As she waited for the electronics to start processing, she hung up her jacket and scarves. Neither machine responded right away, but she didn't worry too much. When the temperatures dropped below zero, like they did at this time of year, the electronics always needed a few extra minutes to wake up.

They're not the only things that need help waking up, she thought as she stifled a yawn with her hand. *Why couldn't Mr. C. be working out of someplace warm, like South America?*

As she turned on the fancy coffee machine to make herself a cappuccino, she glanced around to make sure all was in order. A few magazines sat on the low coffee table in the middle of the room. Two end tables on either side of comfortable chairs held four books each. The elves knew they were welcome to borrow the books as long as they returned them by the end of their Quarter Force shifts.

The coffee machine sputtered to life, and Prerna exhaled with it. Within minutes she held a steaming cup in her hands. She went behind the desk and slid the mouse back and forth across the pad, bringing up her to-do list.

The waiting room door opened, and an elf poked his head around it. Prerna gave him a little wave and blew on her coffee.

"Morning, Jonathan."

"I'm glad you're here," he said. He disappeared for a second, only to enter the waiting room moments later pulling a dolly. "Mail call."

Prerna suppressed a sigh as she pushed back a few of the long black curls that managed to escape her headband. The elf pulled the dolly closer and stood it upright just to the side of the desk.

"Is Mr. C. in?"

Prerna shook her head and turned to the calendar on her computer screen. She clicked a few windows until Mr. C's agenda for the day appeared, took a sip of her coffee, then put it down on the desk.

"He's in the stables. One of the reindeer had a calf last night or was supposed to, anyway."

Jonathan tipped the dolly forward so the oversized bag he'd carried in slid off and pulled a clipboard off the back.

"I guess that means you sign for this then," he said.

Prerna scribbled on the clipboard and turned to face the bag. This time she couldn't stop herself from sighing, although she knew she had the easy job. No matter how late he had to stay up to do it, Mr. C. would read every single letter addressed to him.

"How's the coffee from that newfangled thing?" Jonathan asked, eyeing the steaming mug close to her.

"Really good," she said. "Mr. C.'s thinking about ordering more machines after the holiday rush so the elves can use them."

Jonathan's eyes lit up. A coffee connoisseur, Prerna knew. Rumor had it Jonathan had even worked in the trade somehow, although no one had any more details than that. She wouldn't ask, of course, and no one else would either. Jonathan had only started working at the Arctic Circle a year earlier, and she still remembered the bruises that accompanied his surly disposition when he arrived. He'd fought most of his internal demons, and no one wanted to undo the progress he'd made.

"All right, well, tell Mr. C. I said hello," he said. He gave her a little two-fingered salute and grinned. "See you at lunch later?"

She nodded. "Save me a seat?"

"You got it."

He pulled the dolly back through the door, and Prerna dropped to one knee to start pulling the mail out of the bag. Even though it would create more of a mess than she liked, she started sorting the mail right there on the floor. The letters covered in childish drawings and stickers addressed "To Santa Claus" she put in one pile. The ones that had typed return addresses or asked to be delivered to "S. Claus" went into another.

With the children's letters in one hand and all the grown-up mail in the other, Prerna got up and went to the solid wood door to her right. The entrance to Mr. C.'s office. Even now, more than two years after starting at the Circle herself, she still had trouble believing she worked for one of the busiest men in the world.

She used her shoulder to push the door open and her elbow to hit the switch on the wall. As the boss liked, she left the letters in two neat stacks on either side of his computer keyboard. She glanced around the room to see if she needed to tidy anything, and just then she heard the click of the outer door opening.

"Prerna?"

Rounding the desk, Prerna went to meet the man himself.

"Good morning, Mr. C.," she said. "How's our new baby reindeer?"

Mr. C. unwound the lengthy scarf from his neck and ran a hand over his white beard several times. "Just fine. Beautiful and healthy. The mama's doing well too."

Prerna's smile widened. "Good. I put your mail on your desk, and I'm about to scan the headlines for the day. Do you need anything?"

"Music," Mr. C. said, holding up one finger and then two, "and hot chocolate."

Prerna nodded. "Coming right up, in that order."

She went back to her desk and spun the wheel on the iPod. Within minutes, the first track from a classical album of holiday music floated through the air. Prerna went to the coffee machine next and inserted a pod for hot chocolate. She pressed the wrong button once or twice, and the machine protested with indignant beeps but finally began to percolate.

She returned to her computer and pulled up a few of her favorite newspapers. When she wasn't working her Quarter Force shifts for Mr. C., Prerna lived in Florida. Reading the Orlando papers always made her feel closer to home when she had to come to the Circle for her three months here.

The coffee machine sputtered to a stop, drawing her attention away from the screen. Prerna grabbed a small serving tray from a bottom desk drawer and arranged the hot chocolate and a candy cane on it, then carried it into Mr. C.'s office. Just before pushing in the door, she gripped the tray with one hand and knocked twice with the other.

"Come in."

This time she backed into the door as she took the tray to Mr. C. His eyes twinkled with childish excitement but then dimmed a little.

"No whipped cream?" he asked as he took the tray from her.

Prerna put her hands on her hips. "You know Mrs. C. wants you to watch what you eat. *Especially* at this time of year. It's hard enough with all the cookies and pies that come through here every day."

Mr. C. scrunched his nose in disagreement. "Well... she's not the boss."

"Maybe not," Prerna said, "but she does want *you* to be the boss for a lot longer."

The jolly man grumbled, but his good humor came back as he took his first sips of the hot chocolate. Once again, his eyes lit up.

"Say, that's really good. Let's get in touch with the manufacturer on the 26th and put in that order for about a hundred more machines."

"You got it, Mr. C."

Prerna picked up the tray and went back to her desk. She started scrolling through the news again when the door to the waiting room opened. Two elves, both of them women, came in. One looked absolutely terrified, and Prerna's heart went to her.

"Can I help you?"

The terrified elf managed to stammer out that she had an appointment with Mr. C. first thing. The other elf, more at ease, said the same. Prerna directed both of them to sit down and went back to Mr. C.'s office. Poking her head through the door, she let him know his first appointments of the day had arrived then went back to her computer and clicked checkmarks by the elves' names on her list.

As the day progressed, Prerna kept clicking checkmarks next to the names of the elves who came in and out. In between appointments, she tracked the last shipments of packing material that would hold the gifts tight to one another when Mr. C. flew on the Night Of. She flicked back and forth on her computer between the shipments, the news, celebrity happenings, the weather patterns in various countries, and equipment maintenance. Lunch came and went in what felt like a blink. Prerna knew Final Quarter always flew by, but today seemed exceptionally fast.

In the late afternoon, Mrs. C. stopped in to say hello. She greeted the last elf to leave the waiting room with a smile and insisted that he take several cookies from the plate she held. After a few minutes of small talk, the elf left and Mrs. C. came to Prerna's desk.

"Mrs. C.," Prerna said through a groan, "I can't get the boss to stay on a diet if you keep bringing these by."

"Oh, hush now," the elderly woman said, her eyes sparkling over her small round glasses. "This isn't for Mr. C. I brought these for you to sample. The rest are going in batches to all the cabins tonight. I know how the elves need a little motivation in this last week before the Night Of."

Prerna bit into the perfect blend of flour, butter, sugar, and chocolate. She sighed with contentment around her chewing and nodded her approval.

"Good?" Mrs. C. asked.

"Good," Prerna said with her mouth full. "Everyone's going to love these."

A banner in bright red on her screen flashed twice. Prerna turned her attention to the news site and forgot about the cookie. Her hand lowered to the desk, and she leaned toward the screen as she read the headline.

"Breaking news: Plane executes emergency landing on Utah highway full of cars. Details to come."

Her mouth dropped open.

"What happened, dear?" Mrs. C. asked, coming around the desk. The woman angled down so she could read the screen through her glasses and covered her mouth with her hand.

"Oh, those poor souls," she murmured. "I hope everyone's all right."

Prerna's chest got tight. She didn't know why. No one she knew lived anywhere near Utah. Her parents were in Orlando. Akash...well, Prerna knew he hadn't run to the Beehive State. Still, the tightness wouldn't go away, and she coughed.

Mrs. C. patted her on the back. "Now, now, dear, I'm sure it'll turn out fine."

Just then Mr. C. came out of his office and greeted his wife. He tried to grab a cookie, but Mrs. C. batted his hand away, and a mischievous glint appeared in his eye. His smile extended to Prerna but then faded.

"What's the matter, Prerna?"

She pointed at the screen, unable to form words. Her pulse drummed in her ears, and her reaction disturbed her as much as the news did. Mrs. C. moved back so her husband could read the headline. His brow furrowed as he straightened up.

"Did you know someone there?" he asked.

Prerna shook her head. "No, but I just...it seems like this is...I mean, it feels...important."

Mr. C. looked at her with consideration for a moment then nodded.

"It might be," he said finally, "and if it is, we'll help whoever comes to us the way we help everyone else here: by giving them purpose."

Prerna held his gaze for a moment, and bit by bit her heart stopped pounding.

You probably don't know this, but Santa is nothing more than a glorified chauffeur.

Sure, all the books and movies portray him as a jolly guy who spends Christmas Eve going around the world distributing gifts. That description isn't far off. I mean, Mr. C. definitely has a big heart. He treats all us elves fairly, and even though he works us hard (especially once Thanksgiving hits) he isn't a slave driver.

Oh, yeah, me. I'm Curtis. An elf. No, I don't have pointy ears, I'm not three feet tall, and I don't act like a doofus. I'm right around five-foot-ten and look like your average Joe. Brown hair. Green eyes.

We do have some dwarves—you know, little people with small body trunks and short limbs. They get custom-made counters and work stations. Need a special box to sit on at mealtime. No pointy ears though. Not a single one. Or two, I guess; nope. Just people who are...well, little.

The majority of us elves are normal. We have lives back in the rest of the world when we're not doing our Quarter Force shifts, and there's definitely variety here. Diversity, the affirmative actioners would call it. People from all over, from all walks of life, from every slice of the social strata.

They came to the Arctic Circle for the same reason I did. Working for Mr. C. became the absolute last resort we had. For me, after the plane went down... Well, let's just say every door to all of my other relationships had slammed shut.

And, no, we're not angels in heaven. We're alive, holding down regular jobs back home on the Continents and using our work for Mr. C. as a way to look at ourselves in the mirror again. Except for the fact that we deliver gifts to all of the people in the entire world in a single night, we're nothing like what the movies would have you believe.

Like all that stuff about Mr. C. riding in a sleigh with reindeer? Please. Has anyone stopped to think about the fact that a sleigh can't even support the weight of gifts for *every single person* in the world? And how are eight reindeer supposed to pull a sleigh that heavy?

Yeah, yeah, I know, the sleigh is magic, the reindeer are magic, and so is Santa Claus. Mr. C. makes the job look like magic, but as for the rest of it? I guess it makes for good box office sales during the holidays.

Mr. C. does go around the world, but not in a sleigh. He uses a Concorde. Why do you think they grounded the entire fleet? Mr. C. worked a deal with the FAA and the other aviation organizations across the world. They would let him have the planes, and he would keep their workforce employed.

That part of the deal has worked out pretty well. And Hollywood didn't get everything completely wrong. Mr. C. does use reindeer. They shuttle supplies between warehouses in the compound.

You didn't actually think we made all those toys and wrapped everything in one building, did you?

For those assigned to the Final Quarter Force—October to December—we get to see everything come together on the back end of things, but work for Mr. C. goes year-round. Quality control of products, flight maneuver exercises, vetting of wrapping paper vendors, and paper-work. Mounds and mounds of it. The First Quarter Force deals with most of it, and Second Quarter finishes up (although Mr. C. really prefers that First Quarter get it all done.)

When I came on board eight years ago, I started as part of the First Quarter. If I'd had a choice, I would have lobbied to stay with First. But one thing you learn with Mr. C. is that you don't get many choices. Freedom, yes. Choices, no.

Late May 2015
The Bellagio Hotel
Las Vegas, Nevada

I walked into the Petrossian Bar, grateful to work in one of the classier bars on the Strip that night. No matter where I earned it, I definitely appreciated the extra cash from working as an "on call" bartender. It helped, though, when I didn't have to keep one eye on the door for sketchy-looking patrons while I mixed drinks.

At the Petrossian, I wouldn't have to worry about some guy ducking through the door to push a deal before the cops caught up to him. No, tonight I could watch the high rollers try to outdo one another with how much alcohol they could hold. Having a lot of money didn't necessarily mean a person had a hole in his foot, but it was funny watching some of the rich folks try to drink like they did.

The extra cash would help with upcoming expenses. In a few weeks I'd have to start doling out money to everyone who looked after my place while I worked the Third Quarter shift in the Arctic. People in Vegas thought I went to Hollywood for auditions, and my friends—well, the people I worked with, I guess; I'm not that big on friendships—all of them tried to be polite about what they figured was a major flop of an acting career. Whatever. The point was the people I hired did a good job, and I could trust them not to steal or break anything.

As I crossed the parking lot, I hooked my index finger around the edge of my collar and tugged. The radio jockey said the temperature today would only hit about 79 degrees, but the heat had begun to seep into my skin.

Summer was on its way, and for that, if nothing else, I was grateful for getting to go north. By the time I came back, fall would be poking its head around the corner.

And I would be in Las Vegas this December. Every year was hard, but this year seemed worse. This year, I just wanted to spend the anniversary of the accident holed up in my apartment nursing a bottle of whatever my bartender buddies recommended for forgetting things.

Jogging the last few steps, I went through the door and stopped for a minute so my eyes could adjust. The air conditioning whisked the heat from my face. I saw someone behind the high counter and made my way toward the bar. The man—Stuart, the regular bartender—held a clipboard, and I waited a few minutes while he finished counting bottles and made a note of the inventory left.

"Hey, Curtis," Stuart said, jerking his chin in my direction. "Good to see you back, man. Thanks for helping me out tonight."

"No problem, Stuart," I said. I held out a hand, and Stuart clasped it in a firm hold. "How's it going?"

Stuart updated me on the day's toll so far, and we chatted for a few more minutes while some older patrons stopped in the Petrossian for its famous Afternoon Tea service. Sounds fancy, right? Afternoon tea. The bar at large didn't exactly scream Sin City like so many of the other places on the Strip. Here a grand piano sat off to one side, and the elegant décor featured clean creams and gilt accents in a tasteful way. I don't know much about interior design, but even a goof like me could appreciate the understated approach the Bellagio's designers had taken with the place.

Soon enough the bar and the casino it faced began filling up, and the ringing of the slot machines competed with hundreds of voices. After eight years in Vegas, I'd almost mastered the art of not letting the noise drive me nuts. Some nights—those nights when I couldn't seem to get away from my memories—struggling against the noise gave me exactly the distraction I needed.

The place had just started warming up when a well-dressed man who looked like he was in his twenties took a place at the bar. His designer suit seemed a little off. He kept trying to act all casual, but it came across as exaggerated, like he wanted to hide how uncomfortable he felt sitting in the middle of so many fortunes changing so fast.

"Hello, gentlemen," he said, turning back to Stuart and me. "I trust you're enjoying your evening."

I trust you're enjoying your evening? I thought. *Is this guy serious?*

Out of the corner of my eye, I saw Stuart smirk and then turn his attention to another customer. The millennial sat up straighter when he realized Stuart wouldn't wait on him.

I hope this one isn't higher than a kite, I thought. I'd dealt with my fair share of those ones too.

"What can I do for you?" I asked, placing a cocktail napkin on the bar in front of the man.

"I'll have a Mistletoe Mojito, please," he said.

I stopped moving, and my hand stayed on the napkin for a moment. I stared hard at the man's face, and the man's look changed to one that said he knew me. He nodded once, and I took a step away from the bar and turned my back to him.

He isn't here from Mr. C.'s office, I thought. *He's just some funny crank who thinks it's cute to be drinking Christmas cocktails in May.*

Stuart nudged me with an elbow.

"Hey, you okay?"

I looked at him for a second and then relaxed. "Yeah. Just forgot where the raspberries are."

"In that fridge over there." Stuart nodded to one end of the bar. "Can I pull a bottle of something for you?"

"A shot of rum," I said, kneeling in front of the short fridge and searching for the berries and some fresh mint. "Whatever you've got."

"Contessa okay?"

"Fine."

I stood with the berries and mint and took the shot from Stuart. The man with the napkin watched as I assembled the drink by adding sugar, mint, and seltzer to the rum and the raspberries and gave it a good stir. Some of the cocktail spilled on the work station, and I grabbed a rag to clean the liquid and the bottom of the glass. I placed the tall drink with extra care on the cocktail napkin. The bosses didn't care how much of a mess we made as long as the final product arrived in front of customers clean and dry.

"Ever had one of these before?"

The man eyed the red-pink drink and shook his head. "Not really. I'm not much of a drinker."

My heart started to beat harder than the slots rang. "Then you better pace yourself. Anything else I can get for you?"

The man shook his head again. "How much?"

"Twelve-fifty, please." *And please don't give me what I*

think you're going to give me. Please.

The man pulled out his wallet, dropped a twenty on the bar, and picked up his drink.

"Keep the change," he said.

He nodded at me again, stood, and walked away. After a few moments I couldn't see him anymore. He'd disappeared into the crowd. I snatched the money and examined it, then searched the bar where the man had sat just moments before. Nothing.

I exhaled loud and long and grabbed the edge of the bar. Hanging my head for a few moments, I tried to pull myself together. The millennial had just been a funny crank after all.

I grabbed the cocktail napkin, but something fluttered to the floor from between the folds. I kneeled down and grabbed the small piece of paper. As I read the message on it, my breathing got shallow.

I was pissed. I'd planned everything to work the Third Quarter. I'd lined up people to house-sit my place, to cover my shifts at the regular bar where I work, and to cover the on-call shifts I'd committed to. The money is great on the Strip, and I figure if I can't work it, someone else should share the dough.

Most of all, I'd already begun the huge task of convincing myself to fly again. In the weeks leading up to my Quarter shifts, I started doing daily pep talks about getting back on a plane again. Every single time I came back from the Arctic, it took about a week to talk myself down from the near terror I felt when I flew. I had everything planned, because that's all I had anymore. Plans and my work.

And then this. A note—a note!—that threw all of my planning out the window.

It wasn't long: "Mr. C. requests that you delay your travel plans and prepare to work the Final Quarter Shift this year. Thank you." That was it. I didn't know who had written it—no one had signed it, and there are so many elves who work for Mr. C. it's impossible to know everyone—so I didn't even know who to get mad at. I just knew I had to get mad at someone.

I couldn't even do that, though. When you live alone, have few acquaintances, and no family, you can only yell at the TV, and after a while you start losing that argument too. If I could have, I would have hopped on the next flight up to the Arctic Circle and given Mr. C. a piece of my mind. But I couldn't. I don't fly unless I absolutely have to. And I had a hunch Mr. C. remembered that and used that to his advantage when he changed my shift.

I know what you're thinking. *Why go, Curtis? Why not skip out? Just ignore the note or show up when you were originally scheduled, work your hours, and sneak out of there.*

There's the physical impossibility of that plan, first. Elves have tried to switch shifts before without clearance from the top down, but it's never worked. Never. Every time an elf has tried, something goes wrong. Flight cancellations. Train engine failure at the station. A rock slide that blocks roads. A deep freeze that prevents driving. In the hundreds of years that this entire process has gone on, not once has an elf switched shifts on their own.

You know, now that I think about it, maybe I was

wrong. Maybe there is a little bit of magic going on here.

Second, though, most of us don't try to change our schedules on our own anyway. When it comes right down to it, we just...can't. I've talked to a couple of other elves about this over meals, and all of us agree that we can't get past the way Mr. C. trusts us.

Look, it's one thing if a guy tries to strong-arm you into your work. If he yells and screams or threatens or gets nasty or tries to bully a person into a job, you can sort of argue with that. You can justify undermining the guy's authority by ducking out on your responsibilities.

But how do you justify double crossing a person's complete and utter trust in you? When a person looks you in the eye and thanks you for your efforts from the depths of his heart—and you can see that's where it's coming from and nowhere else—how do you face yourself if you betray that trust? I know I couldn't. And the other elves feel the same way.

So when the note came, I went home that night and let out a scream. I cursed and hurled a pillow on the couch about a thousand times. I wore a path in the floor of my kitchen from pacing. But at the end of it all I sat on my bed, dropped my head in my hands, and knew I wouldn't pack my bags until the fall.

I would work the Final Quarter Force, and not even I could stop myself.

I hefted a duffle bag on one shoulder and pulled the handle out of my rolling suitcase with the other hand as I got out of the airport. I could still feel the imprint in my fingers from the armrests of my seat. The flight left me physically tired and emotionally fractured; I wondered, like I did every time I've flown since the accident, whether that part would ever heal.

The summer had slumped along. I didn't like having time to think, so I'd picked up every single extra shift I could and worked hard at each one. The money had become a... I wouldn't go so far as to say "a blessing." I'd stopped receiving or even believing in blessings a long time ago. But a welcome surprise. Yeah; that's it.

When the air conditioning conked out in my apartment and I'd had to practically haul an HVAC guy to my place in the middle of a Sunday, the guy threatened me with a padded bill. I just shrugged and said no problem. AC in Las Vegas was non-negotiable. At any price. Knowing I could pay that price and not have to spend the next three weeks living on peanut butter and Ramen made me feel a little better.

I guess bad things really do come in threes, I thought now as I boarded the sled mobile from the airport. *First it was the AC, then the transmission in the car. Then that fender bender. Idiot tourist.*

I shook my head and looked out the window at the landscape around me. The change of climate made my bones winter cold, and September still had two days left to go. Back in the Northern Hemisphere Continents most people were pulling out their fall jackets, but here the Arctic temperatures had begun to tumble.

The sled mobile dropped me at the head of the little walkway to my cabin, and I thanked the elf driver. Facing the squat building always made me think of the first time I came to the Arctic. On that day, like today, the freezing temperatures made me inhale a few shallow breaths. Back then, I'd almost felt cold enough to forget my grief.

Almost.

I made my way down the sidewalk and opened the mailbox on the wall next to the door to get the key my roommates would have left there. Sharing a cabin with three other elves wasn't so bad when I never saw them. We each took turns living in the cabin during our Force shifts, and part of the exit paperwork we had to fill out when we prepared to leave the Circle included notes for each other to share any issues with the cabin. Other than the notes, though, I had the same solitude here in the Arctic that I had in Las Vegas.

I started storing my things and checking on the special set of insulated outerwear in the closet marked for me. Mr. C. presented every elf with a new set when they first joined the ranks, and every few years the outerwear got updated. I didn't need to try anything on, but I couldn't help tugging on the brown gloves. Today I let myself think about how they looked different from everyone else's gloves. In fact, they looked almost like the gloves Jo had given me back when we—

No. I wasn't going to let this happen. I wouldn't let myself get sucked back into the past. Mr. C. had asked me to do a job. I'd do it and pick up as much extra work in

December as I could and then leave on New Year's Eve on the first flight out.

The shift change rankled again, and I threw the gloves into the closet. They slammed against the back wall of the wardrobe with a *thwock* and fell to the bottom. I stared at them for a minute.

Mr. C. knows how I feel about being around other people for the anniversary of the accident, and he still... No. I can't do this. Screw him and his schedule changes. He's just gonna have to let me out.

I made a decision. First thing in the morning, I'd request an appointment to see Mr. C. and put my case to him. I couldn't work this December. *Especially* this December. I had to go home and be on my own. That was it.

October 2015
The Arctic Circle

Mr. C. is always generous with his time, but he doesn't have a lot of it to spare. Requesting an appointment to see him always means a minimum of a two-week wait, so even though I wanted nothing more than to hightail it out of the Arctic and get home—even if that meant another flight—I couldn't leave. I told you, it's a matter of principle.

On the first of October, after writing my note and dropping it in the mail, I went to the Assignments Building in my quadrant of the grounds. Mr. C. likes us all to start early on the first day of our shifts. Roll call starts at 9 a.m. sharp. Most of us make it to our work stations by 8:30.

In order to do that, though, I had to know where I needed to go. So I shuffled across the sidewalk and down the street in the freezing winds that sliced through my jacket and sweaters. I had lucked out with the cabin I got assigned. More than one elf had told me they envied how close I lived to the Assignments Building.

I pulled open the main door. A little Christmas chime rang throughout the entire first floor, and I rubbed my gloved hands as I walked inside. The frigid temps made my chest hurt, and I knew I wouldn't stay long enough in the building for my bones to thaw. It didn't help that the sun's weak light wouldn't last long at this time of year.

The elf behind the desk looked away from his desktop screen. "Curtis!"

I held up a hand. "Hey, Mack."

Mack stood and came around the desk, holding out his hand and then engulfing me in a bear hug while he clapped my back. The layers of clothing I wore absorbed most of the impact of his heavy hand, but when he went back around the desk I could still feel the spot where his palm had made contact with my shoulder blade.

"Here for assignments, eh?" Mack asked.

"You got the cushy job this year," I replied. "How do I pull desk duty next season?"

"Gotta work for it, son, gotta work for it," Mack said. "Just give me a minute. This computer isn't exactly a huge fan of subzero temps."

"No problem."

I wandered around the little lobby, looking at the monstrous world map on the wall and the colored pins on it. Each color represented a different part of the drop that happens during the Night Of shift. I'd never done that shift, even though I'd worked Final Quarter twice before, and I knew I'd lucked out both times. After the accident, I didn't fly any more than I absolutely had to. Mr. C. knew that when he recruited me.

"Here we go," Mack said. "Finally got it up and running. Let's see, Curtis...Curtis..."

He ran his finger down the screen. I held my breath, hoping my streak of bad luck getting stuck with Final Quarter didn't include Night Of.

"Gifts," Mack said. "You've got Wrapping this year."

The relief in my stomach made it deflate a little, and I grinned at him while my hands started trembling from a release of adrenaline.

"Fantastic. Where do I start?"

He told me what building to report to, and I thanked him again. After another solid handshake, I tugged at my gloves to make sure they were good and left the building.

As the slicing wind took my breath away, I envied Mack sitting behind the computer in that warm office. I let the door slam behind me.

I didn't know too much about Mack—most of us elves don't spend a lot of time with small talk because the things we might talk about aren't small—but I had to hand it to him. Even at a desk job he managed to stay fit, and at just over six feet he carried himself well. I wondered if he worked out back home when he wasn't working his Quarter Force shifts...wherever home was for him.

I walked past the stables where the reindeer were kept, listening to the sounds of the farm side of Mr. C.'s grounds. Doesn't matter that it's in the Arctic, the elves and the animals on the farm always get up early. I actually didn't mind it when I worked that shift a few years ago.

Mr. C. is pretty attached to the reindeer, as you've probably guessed, and a couple of times during our annual Night After dinner Mrs. C. has joked that she doesn't like her odds when it comes to her husband choosing between spending time with her or the reindeer. We all laugh, but I've noticed Mrs. C.'s look once or twice after she says this. Gotta be tough married to one of the most important people in the world.

When I got to Building 72, I checked in at the front desk. The elf sitting there I didn't know, but that's not unusual. Mr. C. has a workforce of thousands. It's impossible to know everyone. I was actually kinda surprised I'd seen someone I knew at the Assignments Building this morning.

The elf gave me a key and pointed me in the direction of the locker room where I could put my stuff. I picked out a locker and started pulling off all the layers. You think you got it rough in Boston or Maine or even the Yukon with all the clothes you gotta wear to survive? Come work the Final Quarter Force, and you'll think you're wearing friggin' bikinis down there.

It took me a few minutes to unwind the scarfs and pull off the jacket and sweaters. I put my gloves away last. Looking at them made me remember how mad I'd gotten the night before, and my face got warm. Why would Mr. C. have it in for me? He has so many elves to keep track of. There's no way he'd try to force me into something. Maybe he really just needed another pair of hands this year.

I guess I could have thought through that request before dropping it in the mail. I wonder if there's a way to cancel it.

After stopping at the front desk to report the number of the locker I'd claimed for this Quarter, I went through a door behind the desk and stepped into the main warehouse.

It's nice, this picture people have of all the gifts getting wrapped in a single night. Doesn't happen. We start on the first of October and pull eight-hour shifts. When December hits, those turn into twelve-hour shifts. Even then we're usually still scrambling until the night before Christmas Eve. As the world has gotten more materialistic, it's also made our lives busier up here.

I went to the head table and asked the elf on duty what table I needed to join. He checked his clipboard and jerked his head in the direction of the back of the warehouse with a grunt, and I walked down the length of the warehouse watching all the organized chaos. The last time I worked Wrapping in the Final Quarter was six years ago, so I wanted to take a minute to get my head back into it.

Tables about eight feet long stood in neat rows. With them going ten across to the other side of the warehouse, the warehouse holding them ten rows deep, and there being twenty Gift warehouses on campus, there was plenty of work to go around. Which I liked. I didn't want to sit around twiddling my thumbs.

I found my table (fourth row from the front, seventh table across) and steeled myself for the intros. Mr. C. knows it's impossible for everyone to get to know each other and stay friends, so he instituted the "politeness policy." We have to look for opportunities to be polite to one another, starting with the first day of our Force shifts.

Corny, I know. Maybe even a little stupid. But it's Mr. C., so we don't argue.

"I'm Curtis," I said, wanting to get it over with. "Year Eight. Hometown's Las Vegas, Nevada."

"Hey, Curtis," said the female elf across from me. "I'm Sydney, like the city. From Sarasota, Florida. Year Three."

A male elf to my right with jet black hair and small glasses offered both Sydney and me a formal bow.

"I am Sachihiro, from Oshu, Japan. It is my fourteenth year working for Mr. C."

Fourteen years. Wow. And I thought I was a veteran with my eight. Most elves make it to their fifth or sixth year and then fill out their Request for Reintegration. That's a fancy way of saying they think they're ready to just be regular people and not have to work as elves anymore.

If Sachihiro had already been here 14 years...well, I

didn't want to think about what had kept him here that long. When he bowed again, though, it struck me as funny. I tried not to laugh. That definitely wouldn't be polite.

Everyone else at the table went with their intros, and then we just stood around for a few minutes watching the administrators come down the aisles to take roll and hand out assignment sheets. While we waited, one of the elves from the end of the table whose name was Bobby leaned in toward the rest of us.

"I hear the Big Man's thinking of inviting some of the elves to fly with him in the cockpit. Could be as early as this year."

Mr. C. wanted to get elves up in the air? Would we be required to take a test or something? My heart started to fold with anxiety, but Sydney's face lit up like the star on top of the tree. She even squealed a little.

"Are you serious? Oh my gosh, I've always wanted to fly. My parents didn't let me go to flight school; they thought I should do something more financially lucrative with my life."

Sachihiro shook his head. "I do not think I would want to go for this opportunity. I am much happier on the ground."

I couldn't help it; I had to ask. "Then how did you get up here for Final Quarter?"

He got still for a second, and I wondered if I really had offended him this time. Then he smiled a small smile.

"Mr. C. has been generous enough to let me stay here at the Circle. I do not like...flying."

The shock I saw on the other faces probably looked a lot like what they saw on mine. Sachihiro *lived* here? I mean, I hated to fly too, but every time I had to do it part of my training kicked in to reassure me that I would survive taxi, takeoff, and landing, even though I had evidence that survival was a 50-50 proposition. For an elf to live at the Circle, though…everyone knew elves who lived here permanently.

Those elves never applied for Reintegration.

"Well, if Mr. C. does open this up, I'm going to apply." Bobby's eyes gleamed. "This'll probably be the only chance I ever get to do something like this."

"Yeah, but you said it's just a rumor, right?" Sydney said, her excitement fading just a touch. "We have no idea whether he'll ask any of us to train with him. And why would he anyway? Mr. C.'s the one who flies the plane."

She said it with the same certainty we all felt. Mr. C. always flew the plane. But then why would he invite elves to co-pilot? Even if it was just a rumor, it must have started somewhere.

For some reason, I'd never thought about it before, but I began to wonder: how long had Mr. C. been flying? How long had he been…well, Mr. C.? Had someone come before him? Had a bunch of someones?

Was there really magic up here?

Despite how much I kept trying to convince myself that I'd hear from him, I started getting more impatient with the passing weeks and no appointment call from Mr. C. Did it really take the assistants that long to comb through all of the requests? How many requests could there have been so early in the Quarter? What were all those elves in HQ doing, counting candy canes?

When the third week started and no appointment call came by either mail or phone, I broke one of the rules. I sent another request. Mr. C. makes it explicitly clear to every elf who signs on that he'll get to all of our requests, that he'll always make time to address our concerns and talk to us if we need help. But we can only make one appointment request at a time. It's all about trying to control the influx of mail so he can actually get to all of it in time to help.

I didn't care. I'd started enjoying the company of all of the elves on my table—Sydney was cute and fun to talk to, Sachihiro turned out to be a whiz at organizing, and Bobby always went out of his way to help others. But none of them could get rid of the dull feeling that started and ended my days.

I have to see him soon, otherwise...otherwise I'm gonna have to find a way to get out of here.

I sprawled on the sofa at the end of another day, staring at the ceiling. A large picture window across from me framed the frigid landscape. I could see the other buildings of Mr. C.'s campus, and the Northern Lights waved at me from the dark sky. The stars hung high above, quiet witnesses to the show. Some years that depth of blackness helped me forget.

Today, though, the darkness seemed to reach from the sky to the inside of my cabin. The snow across the ground made me think of another day: heavy snowfall, high speed winds, falling forward, screams—

The phone rang, making me jolt and lose my balance. I threw my hand toward the floor to catch myself and scrambled to my feet. The only people who had the number to my landline in the Arctic were the other elves and Mr. C. And even though I sat with elves from my workstation and those I knew from previous shifts during our mass lunch-hour gathering, I hadn't gotten friendly enough with any of them to receive an invitation for an evening meal.

I reached the phone on the kitchen counter on its fourth ring. "Hello?"

"Curtis Sanders?"

"This is Curtis."

"You seem to be an impatient person, Curtis," the voice continued. "You do know Mr. Claus is a busy man, right?"

Anger made my chest puff. "I understand. But it's urgent. I wouldn't break the rules if it wasn't."

"Be that as it may, you aren't the only elf who needs to meet with Mr. Claus. I can offer you an appointment on the nineteenth of November."

The anger burst all around me. "Are you kidding me? I've waited for so long—"

"Then another two weeks won't hurt anything," the elf interrupted. "Unless this is a medical emergency...?"

I couldn't help it: for a second, I thought about lying. Medical emergencies, everyone knows, get top priority. Mr. C. sees the elves who have health issues first, day or night. But even Mr. C. knows not to take a request for a medical emergency appointment at face value, and I wasn't going to start lying to him.

"It's not a medical emergency," I said, wanting to kick myself for my honesty, "but it's just as important."

"Everyone's requests are important," the elf replied. "You can wait until November nineteenth, or I can put you on the list to talk to Mr. Claus after the Quarter is over."

"No, no, November nineteenth is fine; it's good," I said, hating how needy I sounded to the little putz. "What time?"

"You can see Mr. Claus at nine that morning, and you'll have twenty minutes," the elf said. "I would suggest you start planning how to use those minutes wisely."

Yeah, and you could make a plan about where to stick that phone right now.

"Great, thank you," I said aloud. "I'll see Mr. C. then."

"Thank you for your time," the elf replied, self-satisfaction oozing through the phone.

I dropped the phone into its cradle and went back to the couch. The aurora borealis had slipped away, back into the sky, which had gotten deeper in color in the few minutes I'd spent on the phone. The stars beamed on the snow, but tonight their light didn't make me feel better at all.

Mid-November 2015
The Arctic Circle

It took nearly everything I had to get through these last couple of weeks. I'd noticed at some point that Sydney had dimples, but not even her dimples could keep my mind occupied. I wanted to bolt; started thinking about it all the time. When I walked to Building 72 every morning, I thought about how easy it would be to just turn left or right and keep walking. Even Mr. C. couldn't keep an elf from using his own two feet to leave...could he?

I didn't know of anyone who had done it, but we'd all heard the stories about mysterious avalanches and hurricane-force storms that whipped up out of nowhere. I wouldn't put it past Mr. C. to find a way to keep an elf from literally walking away.

Ironically, getting my appointment made it even harder to wait. The sun had stopped rising, so I couldn't mark the days anymore. No matter where I went, in my mind I stayed by the phone waiting for another phone call to say my appointment had changed to *right now.*

This was the first time I'd requested an appointment since starting work up here eight years ago, but I'd seen Mr. C. plenty and joked around with him during Quarters. He would usually come down to the floors and spend some time talking with all of us. I did my best to answer respectfully; my momma may not have been in my life anymore, but that didn't mean I forgot the lessons she taught me when she was smacking me around for the idiotic stuff I pulled as a kid.

She also taught me to appreciate people for the

kindnesses they showed me, and when it came to Mr. C. I did. No matter how much I appreciated the chance to join Mr. C.'s ranks, though, more than anything I knew I had to go home.

I started staying late at Gifts to help sort wrapping paper, be a backup inventory counter, even just to sweep the floors. But the busier my hands stayed, the more my brain kept going back to 2005. To the accident.

It was like I couldn't get away from it, no matter where I went.

I had come to the Arctic to forget everything: the loud screams as it happened, the calls for help, the confusion and pain after it finally, mercifully, came to an end. The new pain that started when I realized everything had changed in the worst possible way.

For the past few years, it didn't feel like shoving cement walls with my bare hands anymore to push away the memories. Once or twice I'd even started to play around with the idea of Reintegration. But the longer I waited for my appointment with Mr. C., the more I realized pushing memories away didn't mean I had stopped remembering.

I could have sworn I'd spent another Quarter waiting for it to happen, but finally the day of my appointment came. Instead of excitement, though, my knees got soft as I walked down the long wood-paneled hallway. After all the waiting that had made my feet drag in the morning walks to Building 72 and around my work station, I should have run down that hall. But on the morning of my meeting with Mr. C., anxiety crawled across my body like bugs.

I arrived at the tall oak door to the waiting room and wanted to knock; instead, I started fidgeting with my clothes. Tugged the points of my shirt collar and each cuff. Brushed away some invisible dust on my pants. Then, before I could talk myself out of it again, I knocked fast.

A few seconds of silence almost convinced me I could run—in the opposite direction—but then the door opened.

"Good morning," said the elf holding the door. "No need to knock. You're welcome to come right on in."

She smiled with kindness as I followed her into the waiting room. Warm light the color of the sun filled the space, and this calmness just spread through my chest. Why would I want to run away? That was dumb. Then I remembered the anxiety from just the other side of the door, and I got confused. Why were my emotions jumping around so much?

"Some hot chocolate, Curtis?" the elf asked.

"Uh...sure."

I sat in one of the plush maroon easy chairs and flipped some pages through one magazine and then another, but none of it seemed interesting. The elf came back with a steaming mug on a silver tray lined with fresh holly berries and leaves. A small candy cane sat on an angle to the left of the mug, and a bowl with whipped cream and a silver spoon sat on the mug's right.

I glanced at the elf as I took the forest-colored mug. "What's with all that?"

The elf's eyebrows rose. "You've never had a candy cane and whipped cream in your hot chocolate?"

I couldn't help smirking. "Not since I was about fifteen."

A flash of anxiety slid across the elf's face, but I blinked and her face had smoothed out again. I couldn't help wondering what she'd been through that had trained her to hide her emotions so well. She took a step back with the tray still in her hands and started to turn away, and I realized I was being a moron.

"Hey, listen," I said, "I'm really sorry. That was kind of jerky of me. Here, I'll have some whipped cream. Just not big on candy canes."

She tilted her head, looking at me for a minute. I realized that if she really wanted to, she could just dump the whole bowl into my lap. She wouldn't have, though. At least, I didn't think so. This close to Mr. C., she definitely wouldn't want to do anything that would kill her politeness brownie points.

Finally, she smiled again. "Sure. Help yourself."

The elf held the tray out to me, and I spooned some of the cream into my mug. I used the spoon to stir, then took a sip. The whipped cream made the hot chocolate silky somehow.

Wow; this stuff didn't come out of a can, that's for sure.

A door on the far side of the lobby opened, and another elf stepped out.

The elf with the tray smiled at her. "Good to see you, Shelby."

Shelby smiled wide. "You too, Julia."

Her white teeth made rows like stars in her dark face. She gave me a friendly nod as if we were passing one another on the street and left. Julia drew the tray toward herself and tilted her head in the direction of the door.

"Mr. C. is ready for you."

I started to put the mug on the coffee table, but Julia said I could take the hot chocolate inside to my meeting.

My meeting. With Mr. C.

I got a little jittery again, and the mug gave me something to focus on. I tightened my grip on it and followed the elf into Mr. C.'s private space.

November 19, 2015
Mr. C.'s office
The Arctic Circle

I tried not to squirm, but the big man wasn't making it easy. He had looked up from his desk when I first walked in and smiled at me. After he told me to take a seat, though, he looked back down at the file in his hands and kept reading.

At least I had the hot chocolate. Yeah, I could have been nicer about the candy cane. But, honestly, I'm a grown man. I don't need friggin' candy canes like some preschooler. And this is Mr. C.'s estate, for crying out loud. We got candy canes like other countries got grass.

So I just sipped the hot chocolate and looked around Mr. C.'s office. Bookcases lined the tall walls. I tried to concentrate on some of the titles, but I gave up after a few minutes. Books were never really my thing; I'm more of an outdoors kinda guy.

The bookcases didn't just have books in them, though. I saw little knick-knacks that looked like they came from different places. Those I found a little more interesting. Before I stopped flying, I'd done my fair share of city hopping—visited enough airport souvenir shops to fill a few shelves of my own, actually—so I could relate to some of these items.

A white cat with Chinese characters all over its head and body and a prominent red collar held up its front paws like it wanted to bat at something. A wide bridge on a framed poster straddled a river; ancient-looking statues dotted the bridge like they'd frozen mid-march. Then came miniatures of some of the world's most famous landmarks: the Eiffel Tower; Big Ben; even the Statue of Liberty.

It made me think, then, that it was possible Mr. C. did more traveling than just the one big trip in December. We saw him pretty frequently, yeah, but sometimes we'd go weeks at a time without spotting him. None of us ever really questioned where he was. I always thought he was just holed up in HQ keeping track of...well, Christmas stuff.

"It's good to see you, Curtis," Mr. C. said in that voice that beat the warmth of my hot chocolate. "I'm sorry it took so long to get an appointment."

"It's okay," I said. "I know you're busy."

"I hope Ronnie didn't give you too much of a hard time on the phone. Sometimes my scheduler takes his job a little too seriously, but he means well."

I waved a hand, trying to make it seem like no big deal.

"So, I understand something urgent has come up."

It hadn't just come up, but how could I make him see that?

"Well, uh, sir, the thing is...I feel like... Well, you know I was supposed to work Third Quarter this year, and then I got your note that you needed me for Final Quarter, and, well...sir, I really don't think I can finish out Final this year."

There. I'd gotten it out. I readjusted myself in my seat, crossed one ankle over the other knee, decided I wasn't comfortable, switched legs. Mr. C.'s eyes pinned me to my spot, and I quit fidgeting. He didn't look mad, just...like he wanted me to stop moving.

"And why not?"

"Sir?"

"Why can't you finish your shift in the Final Quarter this year?"

I looked back at the Chinese cat for a minute. Maybe it wasn't supposed to be playing. Maybe it was supposed to be reaching for something.

"I, uh...well, sir, December's always been a tough time for me. And this December..."

"This December will be ten years since the accident, am I right?"

I found the swirls of froth in my mug from the whipped cream really interesting right then. Back home in Vegas I didn't say the word "accident" where I could hear it. I thought the word a lot. Every single day. Thought about it when I refused shifts at the airport bars or flipped the channels past those stupid chick flicks about two people finally getting together. Those times I flew out of Vegas to come to the Arctic, "accident" rang through my head like the whine of a plane engine. But I never had to say it to anyone.

And Mr. C. had just lobbed it in my direction like a whiffle ball.

"Yes...yes, sir. Ten years."

The corners of his mouth curled up a little bit, and after a couple of moments I realized it was in sympathy.

"Do you really think you'd be better alone with no one to help you through this difficult time? Wouldn't you rather be where you can spend time with friends or others?"

I knew he meant well. But it was so easy for him to sit there and offer me advice. Counseling. I'd had enough counseling. Therapy. Sharing my *feelings* and my *guilt* and why I had a difficult time staying at my old job. I wanted to go home to Vegas and spend the anniversary drunk off my rocker and fight my way through it like I did every year. I wanted to claw through the day and into the night and wake up the next morning proud of myself that I didn't shoot up or snort my way through it. I had that much respect for myself, at least.

"No," I said, "I don't want to spend time with people who don't have a clue what this is all about. No one here knows about my past. They don't know about the accident, and they don't need to know. It's none of their damn business."

Mr. C.'s eyes narrowed just a touch. People have this image of a man bald on top with a long, flowing white beard, a button nose, and small, round spectacles sitting on the edge of that nose. My Arctic boss has all these things. He's round-bellied and loves to laugh and puts his arm around an elf's shoulders with pride when someone does a great job.

But in that subtle shift of attitude, I saw something else: the man who has spent decades honing his schedules and routines to perfection. This man knew a lot about people, and he knew how to get them to do what he wanted. Well, he wouldn't get this elf—no, this *person*—to do what he wanted.

Without a word he got up from the desk and started pacing. After a few minutes he stopped in front of one of the curio shelves. This one had a model of the Taj Mahal. He stared at it while he started talking.

"You know, people in India say that by sharing your grief you can lessen it. I understand the accident changed your life, Curtis. I know it made you a different person—

irrevocably. But I also know that if you go back home now, you will be worse off than if you stayed here."

"And how would you know that? You've never been through what I went through. No, Mr. C., I'm sorry, but I am demanding as politely as possible that you let me go home. I can come back to work both First and Second Quarter at the start of the year, but I need to go home. Now."

Mr. C. stood with his back to me for a little while, and I got worried that I'd gone overboard with the "demanding politely" bit. But I'd had enough fluff and candy canes.

"There's a rumor doing the rounds that I'm going to start training co-pilots for the Night Of shift," he said finally. He turned around, and he smiled at me. The smile made me nervous.

"I'd heard that," I said, and the aftertaste of the hot chocolate went a little sour in my mouth. I didn't want to think about what he might say next.

"It's not a rumor," he said, sitting back down. He picked up a pen and tapped his other hand with it. "I did want to start looking for trainees, just not this soon. But now that the word is out, I want to confirm it for you."

"O-kay."

He stared at me for another minute then smiled. "Tell you what, Curtis. I'll make you a deal. I will let you leave on two conditions. First, you promise to complete an assignment for me on the Continents. Second, you come back to fly with me on the Night Of shift. After that you can take some time off and come back for Third Quarter next year."

The hot chocolate turned into a whirlpool of acid in my stomach. I tried to stare him down, but he didn't seem bothered by it at all. He just sat there, looking at me like he'd looked at the keepsakes on his shelves. Like I was something he could pick up and move to another shelf whenever he wanted.

I swallowed hard. "And what if I don't agree? What if I say that it doesn't matter what you say or do, I'm not coming back to fly with you?"

"Would you be willing to fulfill the first condition at least? Do one Continents assignment for me?"

A Continents assignment. He's going to dump me on some godforsaken island and—

"You have my honor that you'll be close enough to home so that you could drive back, if you're so inclined, for a night or two."

"What's the catch?"

Mr. C. shrugged, palms upturned. "No catch. I want you to stay and get the help of friends and those who care about you. You have a different idea about how to handle the upcoming anniversary of a difficult time in your life. So I'd like to do the next best thing. I'd like you to stay busy on that day. You can do that by doing what you're doing here, which is taking an assigned task and fulfilling it with respect and the best of your ability. Is that too much for an old man to ask?"

I bristled, but it's hard to argue with a man wearing red suspenders over a white shirt and jeans straight from the 1970s. And there were those spectacles. And...oh my god, his eyes were actually twinkling.

"Fine," I said. "I'll do whatever Continents assignment you want. But I'm driving straight home after that."

He dipped his head in a single nod. "That's fine. Thank you, Curtis, for everything you've done here during this

Quarter. I really appreciate all your hard work. This entire venture is only successful year after year because of all the time and effort you and the others put in."

There it was; that gratitude. This was why I couldn't just blow the big man off. I stood up, shook his hand, and left the mug on his desk in the only act of defiance I could come up with at that moment.

November 25, 2015
Building 72
The Arctic Circle

I filled out the last of the paperwork for the night and dropped it into the assigned basket hanging from the edge of my table. The other elves had left a while ago, and I'd finished my assigned tasks two hours earlier. But I wasn't ready to leave yet, so I kept cutting squares of wrapping paper and clipping matching pieces of ribbon to the paper for the next day.

What's wrong with me? Mr. C.'s letting me go. First thing tomorrow, I'm out of here. I get to go someplace close to home, and I don't have to come back after the assignment's done. So why does this bother me?

Since my meeting with Mr. C., I kept getting the nagging feeling that I really hadn't gotten the better end of the deal when he let me out of my shift early. I kept waiting for a phone call or a messenger with a note that said Mr. C. had changed his mind or that operations here at the Arctic had ramped up even more than years past and I would have to stay after all. But no call came. No elf delivered me a sealed envelope.

I made my way to the front of the building and stopped for a moment to look at the enormous map on the wall. It matched the map in the Assignments Building point for point with additional information. This map displayed container numbers with a code following each number. I knew if I looked in one of the dozens of binders sitting in the racks below the map, I'd find the container numbers coordinating with hemispheres and split into countries, regions, states, cities, and even neighborhoods.

Continents residents don't really understand just how complicated this whole operation is.

The other elves and I spend every single day making sure the Night Of will go well. Every job we do, whether we wrap presents or serve meals in the cafeteria, goes towards Mr. C.'s success year after year. None of us have a single doubt about our contribution, because Mr. C. goes out of his way to make sure we all feel invaluable and irreplaceable.

And I had volunteered to walk away from that this year.

It's just this year. Next year will be better. I just have to make it through the end of the year.

After finding Las Vegas on the map like I did when I missed home, I took one more look around the building and left. I went back to the cabin and packed my things, but even that didn't cheer me up. I was going home early, but now the idea scared me.

Something was waiting for me; I just knew it.

Black Friday 2015
The Gateway Mall
Downtown Salt Lake City, Utah

I tried to ignore the holiday shoppers as they hustled around me through the outdoor mall, like they all had to go to the bathroom this very second. A couple of them bumped my shoulder, and when one of them didn't even bother to apologize I knew it was official. I was doomed.

I should have guessed when I boarded the Continents plane the previous day from the Arctic that Mr. C. would pull something like this. When I got on board, a single sheet of paper waited for me on my seat. All it said was that I would work as a substitute driver's ed teacher until the start of winter break. Then a plane would come for me the day after school ended, and I'd spend a few days getting acclimated to the Arctic temps again before the Night Of run.

Either Mr. C. forgot or decided to ignore me when I said there was no way I was coming back for the Night Of. He also forgot to put on the paper where I was headed. I ate my meal on the plane, stretched out on the seat that lowered and flattened to a bed, and went to sleep. The next thing I knew, the elf flight attendant was shaking me awake and telling me we would be landing in SLC in thirty minutes.

When I heard Salt Lake, I'm not gonna lie, my insides started to shake like Jello. The reason I joined Mr. C. was because of Salt Lake. Because of the accident here. After my first shift in his ranks, I got back to SLC and packed everything I owned. I didn't tell anyone where I was going, just that I needed to leave. They all yelled and screamed and cried.

My momma. Dad. And Joanna; Jo.

Momma and Dad loved us, but Jo and I... There's always this talk about some sort of "cosmic connection" between twins. I don't know if that's what we had. I do know that back in college when her dirtbag boyfriend dumped her after she told him she was pregnant, I didn't think twice about what we would do.

The dirtbag wanted her to get an abortion. But she couldn't, she said. Getting an abortion implied she'd made some sort of mistake, and she'd done nothing wrong.

Don't worry, I told her. We would get through it together. And we did.

She moved in with me and had Josh. Those first seven or eight months after he was born were hell. Then it got better. By the time Jo and Kirk got married, Jo and I had life with Josh down like clockwork.

When the accident happened, though, I could feel— actually feel—Jo's heart breaking. And it was breaking because of me. So I had to leave.

I thought I'd never come back. I told myself I'd rather die first and have my ashes brought back in a plane like the ones I used to fly. But here I was. Back again.

And even though now I wanted to hop the first flight back out or take the train or do something, *anything*, to get out, I knew it was no use.

It's funny, when I used to live here Jo and I always talked about how awesome it would be to move closer to downtown. After Josh got a little older, we knew a downtown location would make our lives easier, dropping him off to school and stuff, taking him to all the extracurricular things he had going. I could take the train to the airport for the days I had to fly so she wouldn't have to worry about chauffeuring both Josh and me while she tried to keep her own life together.

In any case, we talked about living downtown. When The Gateway opened right around the 2002 Winter Olympics, everyone got really excited...until we realized it was meant more for the young rocking singles coming to the city. At least we got a great mall out of it.

All of this zipped through my head as I got off the Arctic plane and retrieved my luggage from the carousel, but I had no idea where I was supposed to go. A man at Arrivals had a placard with my name on it, and he told me he'd been hired to drive me to my new temporary home. And then he brought me here.

At least I couldn't fault Mr. C. for the digs; it was an awesome apartment. And I could see the appeal for those rocking singles. Heck, I thought about becoming one myself, which wouldn't be so hard if the mountains looming over my shoulder didn't remind me of what I'd done.

And now here I was in the holiday rush. Since working for Mr. C., the idea of Black Friday has never ceased to amuse me. People want Mr. C. to bring them and their kids all the things on their wish lists, but they can't keep themselves from getting up for those "early bird" hours to buy more just to reassure themselves and each other that they really do care. I don't think even the birds get up as early as the stores open anymore.

I took my time that morning after Thanksgiving. Mr. C. had sprung for a one-bedroom spot on the second floor with a balcony and everything. I threw on a sweatshirt and sweatpants, grabbed my morning coffee, and went to the balcony. It faced a major portion of one of the shopping squares, and I got to see these early-morning shoppers move like ants with sugar crystals across the open area.

I noticed one girl in particular. Couldn't have been more than 17 or 18 at the most. She had her hands dug into her pockets, and she kept her eyes on the ground. Just before she ducked into the movie theater, she looked around like someone had called her name. I watched her, wondering what she could possibly be doing up this early. Didn't teenagers like to sleep in?

I went back inside with my coffee. The girl had jerked her hood closer to her ears before going into the theater, and that told me what kind of weather we would probably have that day. Course, that didn't surprise me. I'd lived here for a long time before I moved to Vegas, probably longer than that girl had been around.

I stopped at the kitchen to rinse out my mug and put it in the sink before crossing the living area back to my bedroom. I really didn't have an agenda for the day. The taxi driver had handed me Mr. C.'s assignment, and it just had the name of the school and what time to show up on it. Nothing else.

The paper lay on the dressing table, and I picked it up again. I knew that school. Josh and Emma-Bear had gone there. Before the accident. Before everything changed forever.

Suddenly I had an urge to drive back to the airport. I wanted to go and watch the planes touch down and take off. I wanted to figure out why they could do it without a problem, and what had gone wrong that day when I'd tried to do it.

Aw, come on, Mr. C. didn't send you here to start beating yourself up. He sent you here to do some good.

Good. What good could I possibly do when I had three days to myself and I had been sent to a city where you could only buy liquor in state-run stores that closed on Sundays? The lines would probably be running down the aisles and out the doors today and tomorrow. Who wanted to deal with that?

I decided to take a nap and get up when the sun had actually risen. Now that I was back in a place where I could see it, I didn't want to leave the apartment until I could feel its heat fighting the winter winds. I set my alarm for a couple hours later and then got up after my nap and took a long hot shower. Then I inhaled long and deep and entered the chaos of Black Friday shopping. I bumped shoulders with people rushing past me to hit the best sales.

And I tried to ignore those mountains.

Monday after Black Friday, 2015
New Horizons Prep Academy
Salt Lake City, Utah

Bright and early Monday morning, I arrived at New Horizons Prep.

I tried to forget the times I'd dropped Josh off, joking with him in the mornings or giving him a talking-to when he acted up. He didn't do it often, but even a great kid like him had his moments. And in those moments, I hated that I had to lecture him like some boring adult.

What I wouldn't give to be boring again.

The back of my throat burned a little, and I coughed into a fist as I entered the school. My feet seemed to know where to go, although a few things had changed. It looked like the administrative offices had gotten a fresh coat of paint. And I didn't recognize any of the staff there.

The receptionist asked for my name, and before I could say anything else she waved me back to another office down the hall.

"Just look for Ms. Rawal's office," she said, "and she'll give you all the details."

I gave a slow nod and read the names on the doors as I passed them. Most of them stood open, including the one for Ms. Rawal. I saw her focusing on the computer screen like her life depended on it, so I knocked on the door.

She glanced at me and then jumped to her feet.

"Uh, Ms. Rawal?" I said. "I'm Curtis. I was told to come down here for the substitute driver's ed..."

"It's Row-el," she said automatically, as if I'd hit the pronunciation button in her brain, "rhymes with towel.

Nice to meet you." She gestured for me to come closer. "I have your paperwork right here somewhere…"

As Ms. Rawal started searching through the messy stacks of papers on her desk, I entered the office and stopped behind the chair. Her frown got deeper as she kept searching. Once, she glanced up at me.

I knew it. Mr. C. got the wrong school or…something. No way would he actually send me back here. Any minute now she's going to tell me there's been some sort of screw-up and—

"Here it is," she said, yanking out a thin file folder. "Curtis Sanders. The background check came back fine, so you can get started right away. Would you like me to show you to your office?"

"My office?" I asked. "Does the driver's ed teacher really have his own office?"

"Her," Ms. Rawal corrected with a sigh, "and she does, because she's also our guidance counselor. Who went into labor right before Thanksgiving."

I narrowed my eyes in thought. "So…wait, I don't get it. Are you saying you want me to work as the guidance counselor?"

"Substitute," Ms. Rawal said, raising a hand as if to stop me. "Just a substitute and just for these two weeks of school before the holiday break. The school's looking for a permanent replacement as we speak."

"But…I'm not qualified for that. I haven't gone to school for it or anything."

"We know," Ms. Rawal said with another sigh. She sounded tired. "But we don't know for sure when or even if Ms. Peterson's coming back, and we're in a real bind. You had some excellent recommendations—stellar, really—

and your former job proves that you can keep a cool head when things get tense, which, with teenagers, is usually every ten minutes."

I scoffed at the idea of keeping a cool head—clearly she didn't know about the accident—but didn't say anything. Ms. Rawal smiled as if I'd reacted to her joke. She glanced through the few pages in my folder, and I wondered all of a sudden what kind of strings Mr. C. had pulled to get me this position in the first place.

"I was also given to believe that this job is some sort of requirement for you in your current line of work...?"

The questioning tone at the end of her words sounded curious enough that I knew she was fishing for details. I wasn't going to give her any, though. I just smiled at her in the most neutral way possible. After a minute, she shrugged.

"I guess we can go check out Ms. Peterson's office now. Follow me."

Two hours later, I sat at the desk and stared at the Mac that sat at an angle facing me. I'd tried to crack the secret language most people seem to know to get the damn thing to work, but all I'd done so far was manage to get two seniors and a super smart sophomore to roll their eyes at me. The sophomore had even smirked on his way out. The dolt.

Guidance counselor, I scoffed. *I can fly a jumbo jet across the world, and Mr. C. sends me to listen to a bunch of whining teens. What's next, sweeping floors in movie theaters?*

I tried to ignore the rest of it; why Mr. C. had sent me here in the first place. It made me think of flight school. Pilots in training would get thrown into simulated situations and have to figure their way out before catastrophe hit. Except here the catastrophe had already happened; I got dropped in after the fact.

Didn't matter. I wasn't going to play the game by Mr. C.'s expectations. I would serve my time in the school and drive south to Vegas the hour after I got out. Maybe I'd go see Josh on the anniversary of the accident. But that was it. My connection with Salt Lake City would end the minute I saw it in the rearview mirror.

Someone knocked, and without waiting for an answer Ms. Rawal stuck her head around the door.

"Your next student is here to see you, Curtis," she said. She ran a hand over her wild black curls, but it didn't keep them from springing back into place. "Her name's Leigh."

"Okay, thanks." I glanced at the computer.

"And by the way," she said in a lower voice, "Leigh's in a mood, if you know what I mean."

I smiled, but the minute she left I deflated against the chair. Teens in a mood and a temp job that didn't include alcohol. Why couldn't Mr. C. have sent me back to the Strip?

Just then the door flew open, and a petite blonde with a sweet face marched into the office. Before I could say anything, she dropped into the chair across the desk and blew some stray hairs out of her eyes. The strands fluttered down in front of her face again, and she shoved them behind her ear.

"What is *with* adults?" she asked. "First I get the most amazing news of my life, and my mother goes ballistic.

Like, totally freaks. You'd think I told her I was an addict. Or pregnant."

Her hands made streaks in the air as she talked.

"Then I get to advanced math today, and we have a pop quiz. Which I *totally* didn't prepare for. I mean, I know it's a pop quiz—okay, I get it—but Mr. Ramirez knows I need to keep my grades up for San Diego! What if I bomb? And what's the deal with a pop quiz right before Christmas break? Who even *does* that?"

I blinked once or twice and turned to the computer. *I wonder if I can order Xanax and start giving it to these kids. Banks hand out lollipops. Kind of the same thing, right?*

"And *then*," the girl continued, her hands still flying around her, "I get here to tell Miz Peterson about San Diego, and I find out I have to deal with a sub—no offense. But, seriously, what is *with* adults?"

"I guess we're just trying to make the lives of teens miserable because that's what the previous generation did for us," I said, adding a weak laugh.

The girl's mouth fell open, and she just stared at me.

"Okay, not a time for jokes, then," I muttered. "Well, my name is Curtis, and I'm filling in for a few days. What can I help you with?"

She huffed in frustration and fell back in her chair. "Well...I just came here to give Miz Peterson the news about San Diego. I mean, U-C San Diego. I applied early acceptance and just got the email last week that I'm in."

She didn't say anything else, and I got the feeling she wanted me to respond.

"Um...congratulations," I said, although I could tell by her face it was a beat too late. "Do you know what you want to major in?"

"Aeronautical engineering," she said.

A smile lit up her face like Rockefeller Center at Christmas, and my skin rippled in recognition. Did I know this girl? Maybe she was one of Emma's friends from before. Was that even possible?

What do you think, diphead? You leave SLC so everyone else does too? There's bound to be a bunch of the same people still living here.

"That's great," I said, again a beat too late. "Um...why aeronautical engineering?"

Her smile shrank bit by bit until it disappeared. It made me think of those lonely lights that got left up after the holidays, the ones that blinked in a feeble attempt to keep the holiday spirit going into the new year. The girl's eyebrows furrowed.

"I want to make planes safer for people."

Her tone told me I needed to tread carefully.

"It sounds like a great choice. I think women make great engineers."

"Really?" she said, crossing her arms. "Do you know any?"

"In my old job I used to," I said before I could stop myself.

She shot up in her chair again. "That's awesome! Do you think you could put me in touch with some of them?"

I started shaking my head before she could finish her sentence, as much at my own stupidity as anything else.

"Sorry, that was a long time ago. I haven't...really..."

She dropped back in the chair with a huff, and I knew I'd already lost her. I glanced at the computer.

"Well, Ms. Peterson isn't here," I said. "Apparently she

went into labor the night before Thanksgiving. But maybe I can put your news on your file for you."

She shrugged with one shoulder. "Whatever."

I grabbed the mouse and swiped it back and forth to wake up the computer. A blank blue screen appeared and told me to "Please wait."

God, do I need lunch. I wonder if that little Korean place down the street is still open. Josh and Emma-Bear used to love their kimchi...

The computer beeped, and I refocused on the screen. I gotta say, it gave me mild anxiety. Although Ms. Rawal had given me the username and password to the school's internal record system, I'd spent way too much time fumbling through all the menus. After I sent the sophomore to class late that morning, I'd decided to go old school and use sticky notes.

This student in front me, though—and the thought of lunch—made me want to try again.

I'm not going to let a friggin' computer beat me today.

"Okay. Um...okay. If you can hang on for just a minute here...let me just...get into the system..."

I started clicking menus on the computer, hoping one of them would bring up the right screen so I could leave a note for Ms. Peterson. A search box appeared.

"What did you say your name was again?"

She rolled her eyes; she must have gotten the memo from all the kids doing the same thing at me all day.

"It's Leigh. But if you're going to look for my official transcript or something, you probably need to look under my full name. That's EmmaLeigh Hawkins."

My heart started drumming in my chest in a steady beat that got louder with every second. My hands got clammy. For a second, I thought I might throw up.

"I'm sorry...what?"

"EmmaLeigh Hawkins," the girl replied, and she crossed her arms again. "But it's not E-m-i-l-y like it sounds. My parents wanted to get all cutesy by combining the names of both my grandmothers. So it's actually Emma and Leigh—you know, those two separate names?— put together. No hyphens or spaces."

My vision clouded, and I could see that day 17 years ago when she was born.

"What if you name her after both grandmothers?" I said, looking at Joanna and then my mother. "This way she's got a piece of both families with her."

Joanna smiled from the hospital bed, and I saw a peacefulness in her face that I hadn't seen with Josh's birth. Then, she'd looked scared and had started to hyperventilate 10 minutes after delivery. The stress, she'd said later. The sheer responsibility had made her want to faint.

No, this time she looked confident and happy. And eager. Eager to start her new life.

"Curtis? Curtis, are you okay?"

I blinked a few times, and my mind brought me back to the guidance counselor's office where I now sat. Leigh— EmmaLeigh; my *Emma-Bear*—had unfolded her arms. She leaned forward in her seat, and her face showed concern mixed with wariness.

"What?" I asked.

"Are you okay? Your face just got really pale."

"I..." I rubbed my forehead, and beads of sweat burst

against my hand. "I'm sorry, I think...I think I'm not feeling that great right now."

She stood up. "Maybe I should just come back tomorrow."

I must have nodded or something, because when I blinked again I saw her standing at the door and halfway around it already.

"You know, you're just a sub, so if you decide to check out early I don't think anyone would care much."

"Okay. Thanks."

She smiled, a full-face smile then, and I knew. I knew beyond what my soul had already recognized, and my brain fired with all the memories and thoughts of the past.

The door shut behind her, and I dropped my head on top of the desk. I'd always known this was a real possibility. Hell, if I had to be really honest with myself, a part of my heart had already figured out that this was why Mr. C. had sent me back to Salt Lake.

I sat there for several minutes absorbing my first encounter with Emma-Bear—*Leigh*, I reminded himself— in eight years. After the shock stopped performing acupuncture on my brain, I started remembering *her*. Those cheeks that used to be so round with baby fat—the reason I'd started calling her "Emma-Bear" in the first place—had thinned out but not too much. She didn't look too skinny like some of those model wannabes.

She had Jo's smile, that was for sure. But she had her dad's eyes. I could practically see Kirk looking at me from them.

Kirk and I had known one another since elementary school and were best buds. He'd been just as responsible for rescuing Joanna after she had Josh. No doubt he'd had to keep doing it after I left.

After the accident, I knew I'd sucked at being a good friend. But, then again, I'd sucked at a lot back then. About the only thing that I'd understood was my work at the Circle.

And I just walked away from that too, I thought. My hands got clammy again. *What kind of genius does that make me?*

Early December 2015
Downtown Salt Lake City, Utah

Screwed. That's what I was. Totally. Utterly. Screwed. Mr. C. didn't want me to spend the anniversary of the accident alone, so he made sure to send me to the one place I didn't want to be for that day. Why?

Well, okay, I knew why. Because I'm a coward. A Benedict Arnold. Do kids even learn about Benedict Arnold these days?

I bet Leigh would know.

I don't know how I did it, but somehow I managed to make it from the school back to the apartment only five blocks away. Screw the Korean restaurant I'd loved, that Joanna had introduced me to. Screw the airlines. Screw Mr. C.

I must have blacked out or something, because I shook my head and found myself in the living room of the apartment. I don't know how I got there. It reminded me of the blackouts I used to have after the accident. The ones that somehow, miraculously, left me physically alive but psychologically contorted. The ones that got me chained to a desk two months after I was grounded.

Look, I know it was just an accident. I had put in my hours of flight training. Up until that day, I had an impeccable record. Kendall used to say that when she and the other flight attendants would find out they were on my team for that day's flights, they would feel relaxed. Relieved, even.

God, Kendall. I sat back on the couch and stared at the ceiling. I hadn't thought about Kendall in so long. Now, it seemed like I couldn't stop the memories from barreling at me.

After I botched the landing, what she and I had also collapsed on the runway. Except we didn't know it in those moments right after. No, we were too busy doing our jobs to make sure everyone stayed alive.

Given the circumstances, the accident could have been much worse. About fifteen people got injured. Only one died. But he was the one who counted the most.

Josh.

I couldn't help it. I curled up on the couch in a fetal position and started to cry. I hadn't done that since...well, since Josh died.

December 17, 2005
Early morning, Hilton Baltimore Hotel
Baltimore, Maryland

Even with my eyes closed, I could still hear Kendall moving around in the room. A hand closed on my shoulder and shook it. I dug a little deeper into the cushy mattress. The hand moved to my arm and tugged.

"Honey, wake up, we're going to be late."

"Hmm?"

"We're going to be late."

I opened my eyes. Every time I saw Kendall smile, it made me feel like I'd just covered myself in a warm blanket. Her eyes were the color of the Caribbean from up in the air, and they glimmered like the sun had just lit them at midday. I reached for her, but she shook her head.

"Unh uh, we have to get up," she said. "We're going to be late."

My arm reached around her bare waist. "Five more minutes."

"You said that fifteen minutes ago. We've got to get moving, otherwise we're going to get in trouble at the airport."

I took in a breath and let it go. "Tell them I quit."

She laughed and pushed my arm back. "Just like that? And you're going to leave a whole plane full of people on the tarmac?"

"You fly the plane," I said, reaching for her leg this time. She managed to get away, which made me push up on my elbow. She did this sexy little walk to the bathroom, looking at me over her shoulder. Her long, dark hair fell to the middle of her back.

"You can't do that, you know," I said. "I'm gonna come after you, and then we'll definitely be late for the flight."

She laughed a little. "Well, if you'd gotten up when the alarm actually went off, we would have been able to get in the shower together."

"So why didn't you wake me up?"

She rolled her eyes.

"Get up," she said, the flirty tone gone.

She went into the bathroom. The shower burst on, and every cell in my body told me to jump in there after her. If I did, though, I knew what would happen.

It's the same thing that happened last night. And early this morning.

I rolled onto my back and laced my fingers behind my head. When we landed after the final leg later that day, I wanted to take Kendall to see the Christmas lights in downtown Salt Lake. The temperatures in SLC weren't much better than they were here in Baltimore this morning, but it didn't matter. I had Kendall. I wanted to be with her, rain, sun, or snow.

Oh, man, do I need to stop watching cheesy holiday movies before sex.

"Honey, seriously, you need to get out of bed," Kendall called from the bathroom. "We really will be late if we don't get moving, and we still need to check out too."

I let out a sigh, and this time I wished I had some time off so Kendall and I weren't running for a flight. After one last minute in the blanket, I threw the covers back and padded across the room. Rubbing the back of my neck, I yawned and went to get ready for what I hoped would be one of the best days of my life. If everything went according to plan, tonight Kendall and I would be wrapping ourselves around each other in my apartment with just her new engagement ring lighting up the room.

December 17, 2005
Cockpit of Flight 87, Midwest America Airlines

"All clear?"

I checked the instrument panel one more time. "All clear." I picked up the microphone and pressed the button. "Flight attendants, please prepare for departure and cross check."

"Are you doing the full route to SLC?" Jared asked.

"Yup. Taking Kendall home to meet the family, and I'm finally going to pop the question."

"You dog, you," my co-pilot said, punching my shoulder. "I hope the weather's not too bad when you make it out there. They say it's looking a little rough."

I shrugged. "It is what it is. I've done worse."

Jared nodded. "And you're getting ready to make the biggest death wish of all anyway. What's a little turbulence compared to that, right?"

This time I punched my co-pilot back. The flight attendants called from the main cabin that everything looked good, and I called it into the control tower. I waved one last time to the ground crew and waited to feel that backward jolt that told me we were in motion toward the runway.

December 17, 2005
Flight 87, Midwest America Airlines
In the air

On the second leg of the itinerary that day, I asked Jared to take over while I went to take a leak. My co-pilot said I should go to the galley to visit Kendall first and made a colorful suggestion of what else I could do in the bathroom. I just shook my head.

Idiot.

After finishing up, I went back to the cockpit and called from there for Kendall to bring me some coffee. A notification popped up on one of the screens with weather information for the destinations ahead.

"Hey, what did you think about that email two weeks ago?" Jared asked. "You know, the one on company policy of pre-determined flight paths in the winter months?"

I shook my head. "I don't know, man. It's a tough call."

"I was talking about it with one of the senior pilots— been flying since the nineties—and he thought it put too much corporate pressure on the pilots. Said there used to be a time when the company would trust its pilots to do the right thing and let 'em decide on their own if they could land safely somewhere."

Corporate pressure. Company policy. Every time the other pilots and I turned around there were new rules to memorize and follow, new protocols to track and not violate. Ever since those bastards on 9/11, everything had gotten so much harder.

Maybe this is a good time to get out, I thought. *I've still got plenty of years left for a good job on the ground.*

Kendall can keep flying if she wants to.

I checked the instrument panel again and began preparing for landing. One more leg, and I'd be on the ground for the holidays with my family. Once Kendall and I joined them, I'd have all the people who mattered most in the world right there with me.

December 17, 2005
Flight 87, Midwest America Airlines
Approaching Salt Lake City International Airport

"I don't know, I don't like the looks of it," Jared said, studying the instrument panel. "Maybe we should circle for a little bit."

I stared hard at the latest weather information that had just come through. It didn't look good at all. But I had to get the plane on the ground. There was the fuel, for one thing, and the next crew had gotten to the airport a little early and sat ready to fly. Every minute they couldn't get in the air meant another minute they couldn't fly on the back end of their own itineraries. Since the FAA's newest regulations about sticking like glue to those schedules, the crews had been a little jumpy when it came to delays.

There had been a memo about that not too long ago too.

"If I use the manual brake, it should be okay," I finally said, my words coming slowly.

After a minute Jared agreed. "That sounds fair. Just gotta watch the tailwind on this one."

I reached for the switch to turn off the auto braking system. "I know."

December 17, 2005
Highway 80, Outside of Salt Lake City International Airport
Salt Lake City, Utah

The screaming rang in my ears, and I couldn't pull in a complete breath. Everything had gone wrong. So wrong.

The plane. Why was the plane on the highway? What happened? Where were we?

My vision started to get cloudy like someone had puffed coal dust in my eyes, and my knees got soft in the middle. I thought I heard someone call my name, but I also had this urgent need to lie down. That urge pushed me to the floor. Then the world went black.

December 19, 2005
Edgewood Park Apartments
Cottonwood Heights, Utah

The phone lay on the floor of the bathroom while I dry heaved into the toilet. My stomach kept pitching, and my brain squeezed tight around one thought. Josh had died.

Instead of running to tackle me at the airport, Josh was still forever. Instead of begging to know what I was getting him for Christmas, Josh was silent for good. Instead of holding up a hand for a high five and then snatching it away at the last second with a laugh, Josh lay in the hospital morgue and I had put him there.

I'd fought the plane through the blizzard. When I brought it down to the ground, Jared started to say, "That was close." Then the plane jolted forward and threw both of us over the instrument panel.

The tailwind. I'd underestimated it. I hadn't made the correct calculation for how hard it would push the plane.

I pulled my knees to my chest, trying and failing to block the images from those final moments.

This awful sense of horror had pressed on my shoulders as the highway rushed toward us. Cars. A bus driver's mouth falling open, then him throwing his arms in front of his face. On instinct my hands yanked the controls, and the plane jerked to one side, skidded, the wheels screaming in protest.

In all the days after, the media called it a holiday miracle. They put out a lot of nonsense about Jared and me being brave and keeping our cool. The plane rushing the highway caused a major pileup and traffic jam, and reporters kept talking about how no one had died.

But now someone had. My family had been coming to the airport for me and got caught in the pileup. I kept searching my memory for whether I'd seen them on the road before the plane skidded and ground to a halt in the middle of the road.

There was no Christmas miracle. Josh was dead.

I dry heaved again.

I lay on the couch; it was like I was on the floor of the bathroom again, feeling those dry heaves. Except this time I just shivered. The damp spot on the cushion beneath my face pressed back into my temple. I'd turned the cushion into a friggin' soggy cracker from crying like a baby.

I don't remember a lot about the two years between the accident and when I started working at the Circle. I'd done everything I could *not* to remember it. But being here now—seeing Leigh face to face—I tried to think about what I'd done in those 24 months.

In the days right after the accident, Joanna came over a lot. She talked and talked. I heard some of what she said. Most of it I didn't. I just watched her mouth moving, tears streaming down her face.

"Please," she'd say to me. "Please try to fight this. We can get through this together, I know we can, but I need you to fight."

My momma came over too. The doctors told her she'd need to have a lot of patience. And she did. For the first time since I was about 9, she put my head in her lap and we sat on the couch while she stroked my hair and talked.

Dad tried his, "Come on, son, you gotta be strong for the family. You gotta be the man" speech. But it didn't work. How could it, when I kept finding pieces of my guilt all around my life?

It didn't matter what anybody said. I knew the truth, and I knew I had to accept it. It was the only way to understand it all. But they kept talking. Why did everyone talk so damn much? They could talk 'til the cows came home. Didn't mean Josh would make it back.

PTSD. That's what the doctors said. It's a pretty screwy four letters to describe the nightmares I had for months afterward. Kendall stuck it out with me for almost a year after the accident, bless her heart, but she finally gave up on me.

I pushed up on the couch and sat there as the memory of her saying goodbye came back to me.

October 4, 2006
Edgewood Park Apartments
Cottonwood Heights, Utah

Kendall stood with her favorite purse hanging on a short strap from her shoulder. Her other hand held the handle of her carry-on, her curled fist tipping back and forth around the handle as if she were kneading bread. I loved her and wanted her and needed her so much. But I also knew I couldn't be the man she loved anymore.

"Say something," she pleaded.

I looked away, forcing myself to focus on the dent in the wall that I'd made one of those nights when my emotions had gotten out of control.

"After I'm done with this itinerary, I'm going back to my apartment," she said, her voice all shaky. "I've put in for a transfer to a new base city. I've got three months left in Salt Lake."

I kept staring at the wall.

"I love you, but you're going to destroy yourself if you don't try to make it past this."

Finally, I looked back at her. Tears started slipping down her face, and I wanted to ask her why she was crying. She came and put her hand to my cheek. The tears started coming faster, and her makeup started to streak. She hated it when her makeup streaked like that. Why was she letting it run in ribbons down her face?

I stayed on the couch into the evening. The memories kept coming back. Joanna coming to me when we were in our senior year of college, terrified, after she took the pregnancy test. Us going to tell Momma and Dad, letting them know we definitely knew what we were doing. (We didn't, not at the time. But, hell, that's why it's wonderful to be young and stupid, right?) Rearranging our whole lives to move in together. Kirk showing up, like the real man that he is, and helping us every step of the way.

Sometime in that year after she had Josh, Jo and Kirk started to get close. Really close. Before I knew it, they were coming to me with excited grins and holding hands like they were teenagers going to prom. They wanted to get married, they said, and they'd come to me for my blessing.

How could I not give it to them? He was my best friend. She was my sister. It made sense.

Emma-Bear came along, and I know Kirk loved his little girl, but Emma-Bear and I were a team. I attended some of the hottest tea parties this side of the Wasatch Front in her playroom. Then the accident happened. Everything changed. About two years later I started working for Mr. C.

Now, as the sky got completely dark, it dawned on me that along the way something had changed again. My heart hurt for Josh. It always would. But it also felt empty. Not the kind of empty that's carved by guilt. The kind of empty that wants to be filled.

But with what?

When I went to bed that night, I didn't have an answer. But for the first time in a long time, the questions didn't bring me nightmares either.

Next morning, December 2015
New Horizons Prep Academy
Downtown Salt Lake City, Utah

I thought I would have spent the night tossing and turning, but at some point I fell asleep. This morning, I was curious. I was also hungry.

I grabbed a bagel and a smoothie from one of my favorite bagel places, happy to see it still served customers, before heading back to the school and going straight to the administration offices.

"Good morning, Curtis," Ms. Rawal said. She smoothed those curls and folded her hands on top of the desk. "How are you today?"

I nodded, feeling a little dumb. "Good. Hey, sorry about yesterday. I don't know what it was. A twenty-four-hour bug or something."

"Leigh said you looked a little pale, but I'm glad you're feeling better."

I half smiled. "I am, thanks. Um, anyone signed up for driving practice today?"

She shook her head, and the turtle shell glasses on her nose slid down. If I didn't know better, I would have sworn she let them slide on purpose to flirt a little.

"Well...good. It'll give me a chance to finish this up."

I held up the white paper bag and the tall plastic smoothie cup. We smiled at each other one more time, and I went through the door with the "Guidance Counselor" slate on the door.

I ate my bagel and thought again about meeting Leigh yesterday. If I stared at the chair where she sat, I could imagine the way she tossed her head and let her hands fly everywhere as she talked. Why hadn't I seen it sooner? It was obvious who she was.

The computer hummed quietly, its screen black, and I got an idea. Wiping my hands on my jeans, I grabbed the mouse and swiped it across the pad again. After several seconds, the computer woke up.

Today, for some reason, it was easier to navigate all the tabs. I put in her name—EmmaLeigh Hawkins—and her records came up. The first few pages showed me her grades, and I whistled long and low.

Damn, this kid's smart.

She'd come in either top of her class or second since middle school. Track star. Honors society. Spearheaded a couple of community service projects in her sophomore year. A member of the Young Engineers of America and started its regional subgroup encouraging girls to become engineers.

Melissa Peterson had kept excellent notes. There was a summary of a conversation she and Leigh had had two weeks ago about Leigh picking up some extra cash during the holidays wrapping presents. I had to laugh at that.

I kept reading and found the notes under the tab "Leigh's Family Life" interesting. I couldn't spend too much time on the lines about Josh's death, so I just skimmed those, but I read through the information about Joanna and Kirk. Kirk taught computer engineering at the University of Utah. Joanna had managed to finish her doctorate in psychology and now ran a radio show about relationships from the basement of their home.

Leigh's maternal grandmother—"who she calls Grammie," Ms. Peterson had typed with a smiley face—lived with the family. Ms. Peterson checked in regularly about Grammie, who led an active social life. Her husband, and Leigh's maternal grandfather, had died five years earlier.

The sip I'd just sucked through the smoothie straw got stuck, and I half choked. Long after the icy fruit drink had traveled down my throat, I kept coughing. My eyes stayed on the words on the screen.

Leigh's grandfather.

My dad.

He...he was—

The door to the office opened, and Ms. Rawal stuck her head around it.

"Curtis? Are you all right?"

I shook my head, held up a hand, tried to use gestures to say everything was fine, dandy loo, don't mind me, but I couldn't seem to stop coughing. Whatever was in my throat refused to budge. Ms. Rawal ducked back behind the door.

Within seconds she came back with a cup of water. Even though I'd just met the woman the day before, she came around the desk and held the cup to my lips, rubbing my back and murmuring something until I started drinking. After a few minutes, the coughing stuttered and finally stopped.

"Sorry," I said, my throat still raw, "think it went down the wrong pipe."

"It's okay," she said, her voice soft. "I think things will start getting better soon."

I frowned at her as I coughed one last time and then finished the water. She gave me a bright smile, pushed the glasses back up her nose, and whirled around. I caught a quick whiff of her perfume—something light and clean;

jasmine, maybe?—and I couldn't help it. I watched her caboose in that gray skirt as she left. Even the black leggings and high-heeled boots looked cute.

Curtis, dude, what's the deal? Are you here to score or help Leigh?

I brought the cup back to my mouth and realized it was empty.

"I'm not here to do anything," I said to the plastic. "I'm here to kill time."

Someone knocked on the door, making me jolt a little in my chair. A tall Asian boy leaned around the door, his body half in, half out.

"May I come in?"

I nodded, glad for a distraction.

"Sure," I said, my voice still a touch raspy.

The boy entered, and everything about the way he came in said "fluid." He didn't walk across that floor. He glided over it. He was wearing the same uniform all the boys in the school wore—black pants, white collared shirt, black tie, maroon sweater vest—but on him the uniform didn't hang. It made the kid look like he belonged at a black-tie event. He lowered himself into the chair opposite me.

"Hi," the boy said, and just that one word, in its respectful tone and with the right amount of deference, told me this kid probably had never screwed around in his entire life.

"What can I do for you?" I asked. I folded my hands on top of the desk and tried to look like someone capable of giving mildly sensible guidance.

"Um, so, my name is Aaron. Aaron Young," he said. "I need some...advice."

Now that he sat closer, I could hear a touch of a lisp. I also noticed a scar that ran up from the middle of Aaron's top lip in a diagonal line to just below his left nostril. The boy smiled a lot, though, and his smile made it easy to forget that scar or the way the S sound cradled his words.

"Okay, well, I'll do my best," I said. "I know you were probably looking for Ms. Peterson, but I'm what you got. So, what's up?"

The boy sat back in the chair, at ease, and crossed his legs at the ankles.

"Well, I really want to...that is, I've been...I've been taking ballet lessons since I was seven, and I really want to do what I can to make it as a professional dancer, and my parents kind of support me but they also want me to get a real degree—" he put air quotes around those words "—and just yesterday I got an email from the Houston Ballet Company that they want to sign me for a two-year contract and I really want this to be the start of something and—"

"Whoa, whoa," I said, holding up a hand. "Slow down, Aaron. Breathe. I need you to back up a second."

Aaron stopped right away and blinked, his face getting all serious and ready to concentrate.

"This thing with the Houston Ballet Company. You had to audition for this, I'm guessing?"

Aaron nodded.

"So did your parents know about the audition?"

Aaron dipped his head from side to side. "Sort of. There were two other dancers who auditioned too, but I think they did it because our ballet company director wanted those dancers to get the experience. But the director knows that I'm really serious about this. She's even talked to my parents, but they kind of... Well, see, they're my adoptive parents, and my dad's this big athlete, and he says he's proud of me, and I know he is, but I think that some part of him thinks..."

"That ballet's for wusses?" I said.

Aaron nodded and examined his fingers. "I know what the stereotypes are. But dance is...it's my whole life."

"And what would happen if you couldn't dance?"

Aaron's head snapped up and started shaking a hard no. "There's no way. I'm always going to be dancing. No two ways about it."

I scoffed. "And you're basing this on your years of vast life experience, right?"

A grin crossed Aaron's face. "All right, you got me there. But what do I do?"

I stared at him for a minute. What should he do? How the hell would I know? What did this kid think I was a...a...guidance counselor? No. I wasn't a guidance counselor. I was a washed-up airline pilot who spent most of my year tending bar and part of it working at the Circle.

I opened my mouth to tell Aaron I didn't have the first damn clue what to do when someone knocked on the door. Ms. Rawal.

"Hi, Curtis. Leigh's here to see you again. I just wanted to let you know. And Aaron probably needs to get back to class soon."

"Thanks," I said.

Hearing Leigh's name made me think of Josh. What if Josh had wanted to dance? Or play football? Or anything else? What would I have done to help make sure those dreams came true?

It didn't matter, because he'd never get the chance to

find out. In some twisted way, it didn't even matter that Josh wasn't here right now. Aaron was. And he was the one who needed advice.

"Why can't you dance and get a degree?" I asked.

Aaron smiled, the kind of smile a parent gives a kid when they're about to explain something hard. "Dance is a full-time discipline in and of itself. I'll have to be in the studio all the time and push myself if I want to make it big."

"And what exactly does 'make it big' mean to you?"

"It means dance as the principal in a ballet company."

"And when you get injured and your part goes to someone else, what are you going to do then?"

He shook his head with that patient smile again. "I won't get injured. I'm always very careful."

"So you plan to live and eat and sleep in the dance studio then, is that it?"

Aaron opened his mouth, but his expression changed. He closed his mouth again and frowned.

"See, Aaron, here's the thing," I said, getting up. I started pacing behind the desk. "You could have an amazing career as a ballet dancer and be one of the greats. Or you could go to Houston and fall off the curb when you go to get the mail, break your ankle, and never dance again. Injuries can happen anywhere, at any time."

"So you're telling me I shouldn't dance at all?" Aaron said, the words coming out of his mouth like a mule refusing to go anywhere.

I shook my head. "I'm telling you that you should go to Houston and dance for as long as you want. But you should also get a college education. Dance is a physical thing. At some point your body's gonna give out on you. It may not happen right away," I said, holding up a hand as Aaron opened his mouth to argue, "but eventually even the most careful athletes slow down and can't play anymore. Your education will last you until the day you die."

Aaron fidgeted in his chair; he looked like he couldn't quite find a comfortable spot.

I sat down again. "All I'm saying is to keep the door open on education too. Go home, talk to your parents, tell 'em you got into Houston, and then follow that right up with, 'But I want to explore my education options while I'm out there.' Then go out and actually do it. You'd be surprised at how supportive they are then."

Aaron kept frowning. After a moment he stood up.

"All right," he said. "I'll, um...think about it."

I held my hands up, palms out. "That's all I'm saying."

"Thanks."

"You're welcome."

Aaron left, and Leigh walked in. Her chin-length blonde hair swished back and forth as she followed Aaron with her eyes and then turned back to me.

"What's he so upset about?" she asked, hooking her thumb over her shoulder. "He's an only child too, and he's got, like, the best grades ever."

My brain tripped over the description. Of course Leigh thought of herself as an only child now. Why wouldn't she?"

She dropped into the seat Aaron had just left and crossed one leg over the other. "Anyway. So. Are you feeling better?"

I nodded. "Yes, thanks. And I finally managed to figure out the computer, so I put a note in there for Ms. Peterson about U-C San Diego."

"Great," Leigh said. "Now all I need to do is to send them a hard copy of my transcript from first semester, and it's official. My mother can't get on my case about it. She has to let me go."

"Why, uh...why doesn't she want you to go?" I asked, leaning back in the chair, knowing I probably wasn't looking as casual as I thought.

Leigh rolled her eyes. "She's freaked about me leaving town. Says she doesn't want to lose any more family. I mean, I get it—totally, I do—but I can't live my life in a fish bowl, right?"

I wanted to ask the question and not ask it all at the same time. Finally, I decided to go for it. If I didn't, it would eat at me for the rest of the day.

"What do you mean, lose any more family?"

Leigh looked at me for a minute, but I couldn't read her expression.

"My older brother died when I was seven," she said, the words neutral, "and then my uncle—my mom's brother—just kind of...well, you could say he sort of checked out of the family. It was hard, because we were all super close before that."

"Oh. I mean, I'm sorry to hear that."

Leigh shook her head and waved her hands a little. "No, really, on most days it's not bad. She's, um...well, Mom's done an amazing job of pulling herself together. And she helps so many other people now by counseling them. Kind of what you're doing, huh?"

I chuckled. *Sure, that's what I'm doing here.*

"Anyway, she says I should go to the U like everyone else because Utah has engineering too, and why can't I stay in town like all the other kids do, blah blah blah. And I told her I need to get out. That I feel like I'm living under a microscope."

She stared down at her hands and played with one of the cuffs on her long-sleeved blouse.

"I told her about my early acceptance on Thursday. We kind of had a big fight about it during Thanksgiving dinner. And we had another fight over the weekend. So I've been avoiding her since then. Which isn't hard, what with all the work left for the winter formal coming up, and then we've got our annual homeless shelter food drive, and... I guess I've just...kind of been hoping that she'll get it. My dad is totally on board with this—he was the one who signed where you need parental consent and stuff— but Mom's been a basket case."

I listened to this description of Joanna—the "smart" twin, the one who seemed to have everything together— and knew in my gut as if she'd told me herself.

I knew right then that she hadn't been able to let go of her guilt either.

"Well, um... I think... I think, if your dad's on board with this, then you've just gotta give your mom some time to come around."

Leigh shook her head again. "I don't think she will. I even tried to talk to her about how responsible I can be about this whole going-away-to-school thing. I've taken care of all the paperwork on my own. That was another reason why I needed to come to Miz Peterson, to let her know about the transcript. It has to be postmarked by December thirty-first. But Mom's all crazy right now, and she won't listen to what I have to say."

I searched my memory for anything I could offer to Leigh as advice on my sister. But I hadn't talked to Jo in so many years. What if things had changed beyond what my memory could help with?

"Maybe your mom just needs some time," I said slowly. "I would say keep trying to talk to her. You've got winter break coming up in a couple of weeks. Maybe just spend some time with her then. You know; show her pictures of awesome San Diego beaches. Remind her that it's warm in California in December."

The corners of Leigh's mouth turned up just a little, and her shoulders relaxed a little.

"Maybe. Thanks. And I'm sorry, by the way, about the way I just barged in here yesterday."

"It's cool," I said, and then I smiled. "Do kids still say that these days? It's hard to keep up with all the slang."

She laughed. "Yeah, kids still say that."

I didn't see Leigh in the office again after that, but I couldn't stop thinking about what she'd said. I also couldn't stop thinking about Jo. My sister. The "daredevil" of the two of us.

She always used to come up with these wacky ideas, these pranks and things, that we'd pull off together. Some of them actually came through—I don't think to this day Mr. Sullivan knows we were the ones who put the little cups full of green-colored water in the shape of an enormous shamrock on his driveway—but most of the time we'd get caught. Didn't stop Jo. By the next week she'd be knee-deep in another plan.

She was even the one who bullied me into going to flight school. She knew I wouldn't have the guts to tell Momma and Dad that's what I wanted to do. So she dropped it on them at dinner one night.

I wonder if she'd ever told Leigh that story.

When Jo got pregnant and came to live with me, I told her I would forget about flying and get a desk job. It'd be easier, I told her, if I could stick around and help her. That way she wouldn't have to worry about quitting school herself.

She nearly took my head off with the way she yelled that no way in hell was I going to give up on flying. Because she knew what it meant to me to be able to get up in the air. I'm not going to go off on some fru-fru description of what it felt like to be above the horizon, but up there the world made sense.

Ever since the accident all of that had been grounded for me. Not much made sense anymore. Maybe I wasn't the only one who felt that way, though.

For the rest of the week, I thought about Leigh. And Jo. And even Kirk. Sometime on Saturday I suddenly remembered that he'd come over a lot right after the accident too. But he didn't do any talking. He just sat.

Come to think of it, those were some of the most beneficial conversations I had about the whole thing. That's what made us best friends back then. Jo was my sister—we had something I didn't have with anyone else in the world—but Kirk was my guy.

Hell, I missed 'em. I missed all of 'em. Even my dad...

On Sunday morning as I lay in bed, I heard the chimes of the Salt Palace, the ginormous Mormon church that dominates downtown. Something about a Sunday morning makes a person think about life, you know? Think about what we're doing here. Why we were even created or evolved or whatever you wanna believe. People have a lot of theories about it all, but no matter what you claim you believe, one thing's for sure: death is real, and it's final.

Josh was gone. My dad was gone. How many more family members would I lose? Would my momma be next? If I walked away from this Continents assignment and went back to my life in Vegas, would I ever know if—when—Momma died?

Would I be okay living like that for the rest of my own life?

Maybe that's why Mr. C. sent me back. To show me that I needed to move past the accident. But how could I take ownership for what I'd done wrong and move past it all at the same time?

On Monday morning I woke up and knew in my bones, like I know every year, that the anniversary was coming up. I looked at the calendar on my phone, even though the day had branded itself into my brain weeks ago. Yup. The anniversary was on Thursday.

I also knew I needed to do something I hadn't done in 10 years. I needed to visit Josh. Needed to go to the cemetery and tell him how sorry I was. Needed him to understand why I left. Once I did that, I'd be able to leave Salt Lake knowing I'd done everything I possibly could for my family.

By the time I got to New Horizons Prep that morning, my chest felt a little lighter. All the previous years in December I'd walk around with this mountain on my shoulders, and nothing except some choice libations could dissolve it.

This year, though, the mountain had shrunk to a boulder. Still heavy enough to weigh on my life but not as much as before.

Funny enough, not a single kid wanted to schedule a practice drive for that entire week. All of them wanted to talk. I spent the week chatting with the seniors who streamed in and out of the office with updates on their college acceptances and rejections. One girl, Rebecca, collapsed in tears and cried for a solid 15 minutes before Ms. Rawal could convince her to stop. Apparently this one had her heart set on Johns Hopkins for early acceptance, and Hopkins had kicked her application back.

"You don't need 'em," I said.

Ms. Rawal frowned at me over Rebecca's head while handing her more tissues.

"What I mean," I said, realizing how idiotic I sounded, "is that there are plenty of other great universities out there. I'm sure they'd be glad to have you."

"But I've barely started my common application! How am I going to get everything together in time?" Rebecca wailed.

Geez, did all girls sound like cats being run over when they got worked up? I didn't remember Jo ever making a fuss like this. I opened my mouth with a snarky comment, but I swear Ms. Rawal saw it in my brain. I closed my jaws and tried again.

"You're going to make a list of what you need to do for the common application and then look at your schedule... planner...thingy and do one or two things on your list every single day until the damned thing is finished," I said drily. "When's the deadline?"

She sniffled, and her shoulders hitched a few times. "Decemb...December thirty-first."

I rolled my eyes. At least Leigh had her stuff together. I bet Josh would have had it all together too.

"So that gives you, what, two weeks, right?" I asked. "Two weeks is something. Do you really wanna go Ivy League?"

She nodded and blew her nose.

"Do you have the grades and stuff to get in?"

She nodded again.

"And you fill out this common application online and it goes to all of 'em?"

One more nod.

"Then stop acting like a third grader and get it together," I said, throwing my hands in the air. "You can do this. You're not flying a space shuttle, for crying out loud!"

Rebecca sniffled a few more times, but she'd stopped crying. She didn't say anything for a few minutes, and I got worried that I'd offended her. She was a little tubby, if I have to be perfectly honest, and she wore these huge round glasses that made me think of that wizard kid.

"You know," she said in a small voice, "you're right. I *can* do this. I should...I should just start making a list, like you said. In fact..."

She pulled out her smartphone and started scrolling. Grabbing one last tissue from the box in Ms. Rawal's hand, Rebecca wiped her tears, pushed those round glasses up on her face, and tugged at the bottom of her gray sweater vest.

"Thanks, Curtis," she mumbled. "I really appreciate it."

"Any time," I said as she turned and left the office. Ms. Rawal and I exchanged a smile. *Teenagers, huh?*

"Nicely done, Curtis," she said, crossing her arms. "Have you ever thought about going back to school to get a degree in education? You might actually have a knack for this."

I chuckled. "Thanks, Ms. Rawal, but come Friday I'm out of here. I gotta head home to Vegas and get back to my regular job. But I am glad I got to work with the kids this week and help 'em out. I think most of the time they're smart enough to figure this out on their own. They just need someone who isn't blind with hormones to point stuff out to them."

I smiled again at her, but she didn't smile back. Her eyebrows formed a V, and she looked worried.

"So you're leaving town this weekend?"

"I have to," I said. "I've got a whole life waiting for me in Vegas."

The words sounded funny to me, even though they'd come out of my own mouth. *Did* I have a whole life waiting in Vegas? Or was it just an empty apartment and a list of bars that needed someone to work the late shift every now and then?

I shook my head. I'd made up my mind, and I knew it was the right thing for me. I needed to go home.

Ms. Rawal didn't say anything else. She just left the office, and I turned and looked at the desk.

Is it really the right thing for you? a voice whispered from somewhere inside my head. *Is it the right thing for the family you're leaving behind?*

Shut it, I answered. *I'm doing what's best for everybody. They don't need me. Jo's got her life together. Kirk's doing well. Momma's living with them, so she's not alone. And Leigh's gonna be an amazing engineer. So everything's fine.*

Is it? the voice asked again.

I shook my head hard and ignored the nag inside of it.

I lay on my back in bed, staring in the direction of the ceiling even though I had a hard time making out the details of the patterns in the morning light.

Josh died today, I thought.

It was the same thought I had every year on the morning of the anniversary. Every year I woke up in the early-morning hours—around the same time Joanna had called from the hospital and barely said the words before she started gagging. Every year I stared at the ceiling wherever I was and reminded myself that because I'd made the decision to land the plane without any help, Josh had died.

Twice I'd been at the Circle for the anniversary, and, god, what I wouldn't have given for a drink both times. Of course, Mr. C. doesn't allow substances of any kind at the Circle. Any elf caught with anything like that...well, let's just say they don't make that mistake twice.

This year my throat burned again. My eyes stung in the corners, and tears started sliding out. I could hear the tears landing on my pillow, making these little puffing sounds like someone trying to catch their breath.

I closed my eyes, but I didn't see nine-year-old Josh standing at home plate with a bat. This year I saw Leigh. Her short blonde hair, those hazel eyes that lit up when she'd laughed at me using slang. The little girl who had convinced me to wear a feather boa at the last tea party we'd had, the day before I decided I needed to leave Salt Lake forever.

Then, I'd thought I couldn't do this. I couldn't go on playing pretend like nothing had gone wrong. I'd been the one to support Joanna's decision to keep Josh, and I'd been the one to take him away from her.

But today all I could see was Leigh. *Emma-Bear*, I thought, suddenly laughing at a memory that popped in my head of her posing with all her stuffed animals crowded around her.

You call me Emma-Bear, she'd said like the wise five-year-old she was then. *Now I really am a bear!*

I'd laughed so hard, and she'd grinned. Those chubby cheeks got pink, and I'd snapped the picture. For the longest time I'd kept the photo on my fridge.

I blinked, and my tears slowed down. Where was that picture now? Did I still have it somewhere? Did Jo?

Probably not. Jo had made it clear how hurt she was when I told her I was leaving. Most likely she'd gotten rid of all my stuff.

I shuddered and put the heels of my hands to my eyes.

"Come on, Curtis, get it together," I said. "Just make it through the day, and tomorrow you're outta here."

I pushed myself off the bed and power-walked to the bathroom to get into the shower before I could do any more thinking.

Later in the morning I listened to a junior drone on and on about why he didn't need to apply to college at all, about how he would join the anti-college movement and be making a six-figure salary inside of five years. I tried to ask a few questions about what job would give him that kind of pay, but when I didn't get any straight answers, I just recommended the student talk to Ms. Peterson when she came back after Christmas break and signed the hall pass.

Even the junior with no life plan made me think of Josh. How Josh never had the chance to say he was joining an anti-college movement—although I knew Jo, Kirk, and I would have sent Josh packing to college no matter how much he argued against it. But I wished for a few minutes that Josh could have at least fought for it.

I looked at the clock. Fifteen minutes to noon.

That's it, I'm going to see Josh now, and after that I'm going back to the apartment and leaving. I can't do this for another day.

I grabbed my coat off the stand that Melissa Peterson had so thoughtfully placed in a far corner of the room and wound my scarf around my neck a few times. After making sure I had my phone and keys, I turned off the light to the office and went out the door.

"Ms. Rawal, I think I'm going to head out early today. I've got a long drive ahead of me tomorrow, and I need to go start putting my stuff together."

She shot out of her chair, her black curls bouncing. "You're leaving? I thought you weren't going until Saturday."

I scrubbed my hair. "I know, but, um...something's come up. Besides, tomorrow's the last day before break, and I figure most of the kids probably won't care about school stuff anyway, am I right?"

She tried a smile, but it looked off. Whatever. I couldn't

stand here and try to solve the problems of a kooky secretary—even if she did look really good in her slacks today. I had to go.

"What if someone comes in after lunch with a question?" she asked.

"Can't you handle it?"

"I guess technically I could," she said slowly, "but the principal asked me to do some stuff for him this afternoon since his secretary is out with the flu."

"Well, just text me then," I said, scribbling my cell number on a pad on her desk. "I have to go."

She looked at the paper for a minute that lasted an infinity and then nodded. I left the building and took in a deep breath. That mountain on my chest had come back.

December 19, 2015
Day of Josh's death anniversary
Downtown Salt Lake City, Utah

I drove through the streets of the city like I was seeing them for the first time. It looked like everything had changed, but nothing had, I guess. The latest snow to fall had been pushed against the edges of the streets. It lay in heaps of browns and grays, like a mangy dog a guy kicks to the curb.

I headed to the Salt Lake City Cemetery in that trendy part of town known as The Avenues. People look at The Avenues these days as a way to take a bite out of some hot real estate that offered owners historic homes at twenty-first century prices. Jo and I had talked about buying a house in The Avenues, back before she and Kirk got married. Today I was so glad we didn't go through with it. Knowing I was responsible for Josh's death had driven me out of SLC. Living that close to his grave would have driven Jo insane.

From Main Street I turned onto the minor roads that would lead me to Olive Street. The side where Josh was buried. I slowed down, took a deep breath...and kept driving. I couldn't do it. Not yet.

Come on, just get on with it. This is why you came here.
Why Mr. C. sent you here. Get on with it, and you can go
home and start letting go of your guilt.

I circled the cemetery, came back to Olive Street, and brought the car to a stop at the intersection. A car behind me slowed down and stopped. One good thing about cemeteries is that people don't rush you. They don't honk their horns or give you the finger. They probably need time to bring it all in too.

Finally, I made the turn and let the car crawl down the street. And then I saw it. Or them, I guess. Someone had beaten me to the punch today.

There was Leigh with three other people. After I squinted to make sure, I knew who they were.

Jo stood there with a poinsettia plant in her hand. Kirk had his arm around her, and Momma—my dear sweet momma, who I hadn't seen in eight years—had her arm looped through Leigh's. My sister took a couple of steps toward the headstone, and I noticed that she was wearing the red winter coat I'd bought her the year before the accident. She'd made a joke when she opened the box, but the coat had come from this hip store in Minnesota and I could tell she was excited about getting something a little different from what we would get here in SLC.

She still had the coat. Maybe she hadn't gotten rid of everything of mine after all.

Jo's shoulders started shaking, though, and after a minute her body started to fold. Kirk rushed forward, and he guided her in an upright position again. Momma came to them, pulling Leigh's arm. After a minute, they were all standing there in a group hug.

The mountain on my chest threatened to collapse into an avalanche, and more than anything I wanted to jump out of the car and run toward all of them so they could buffer me from everything falling on my head right then.

My hands stayed on the steering wheel. After eight years, would they really accept me? Would they want me back?

Just then my phone beeped a text. I fumbled with my

gloves—the ones Jo had given me for a birthday so many years ago; the gloves that looked so much like the ones that Mr. C. had given me at the Circle. After a few moments of tugging, I got the gloves off and dug my phone out of my pocket.

Hi, Curtis! This is Ms. Rawal. Got that transcript. You can give it to Leigh in school tomorrow. Was absent today.

Transcript? What transcript? I texted.

The one you emailed me about, the phone replied, and I could almost feel her confusion through it.

Never emailed you about a transcript, I wrote.

I waited a few minutes but didn't get anything back. Jo, Kirk, Leigh, and Momma had managed to break the huddle and go to Josh's headstone. I could see Jo talking and wished I had the guts to go stand with her. Momma said something, then Kirk, and lastly Leigh. They shared another group hug and then moved toward a navy sedan.

A bicycle bell rang from my phone. Email. The hairs on the back of my neck started to prickle, but I ignored them and swiped several times across the screen. Sure enough, there was a forwarded message with my name on it asking Ms. Rawal to get Leigh's first semester transcript ready so Leigh could mail it to U-C San Diego before the end of the year.

Damn. Damn, damn, damn.

This had Mr. C. all over it. I'd come to SLC with no intention of letting anyone bully me into anything. But Mr. C. had, once again, made my choices for me.

I sighed long and loud, started the car, and headed back to the school. If I was going to do this, I wanted to get it over fast. Like ripping off a Band-Aid.

December 19, 2015
Day of Josh's death anniversary
New Horizons Prep Academy
Salt Lake City, Utah

I circled the school parking lot for a third time before finally finding a spot. I didn't bother to check whether the car was straight between the yellow lines. I just got out and jogged to the administration offices.

During the drive from the cemetery, this frustration on a slow burn started building inside me. Why the hell couldn't anyone just leave me alone? Did I really have to take care of Leigh's transcript? Why couldn't Ms. Rawal give it to her?

That question didn't occur to me until I stood outside the office, and I wanted to storm in and ask her why I had to get dragged back into something that was really just a temp job to begin with. But when I went to her desk, her chair sat empty in front of a dark computer screen. I went into the guidance counselor's office to see if I'd missed anything. Sure enough, an envelope sat on top of Melissa Peterson's desk. A Christmas-themed sticky note on top said Leigh's transcript was inside, and it ended with this dumb smiley face next to a cheerful "Thank you!"

"Oh, for the love of..." I muttered. I wadded up the note and threw it in the trash. Then I grabbed Leigh's transcript and marched back out of the office.

This would end today. Now. Mr. C. may have tried to put something fuzzy and sentimental in motion, but I wasn't about fuzzy. I would finish this before the day was out.

I followed the traffic and cussed at the windshield when the cars didn't go warp speed like I wanted them to. Finally, finally, I made it to Jo's neighborhood. The car practically drove itself down the streets with bare trees. A wind did its best to push the half-dead branches in different directions, but the trees didn't budge. That's how I needed to be: immovable. Just like the mountains around us.

I pulled into Jo's driveway, got out of the car, slammed the door, and stopped.

What was I doing? I shouldn't have come here. I should have gone back to the apartment, packed the few clothes I had with me, and driven south at about 90 miles an hour.

My ear caught the sound of paper crinkling, and I realized I still had the envelope for Leigh. For just a minute, I thought about dumping it somewhere. Just tossing it. But I couldn't. Not after everything she'd done to get into college. I may have been a jerk to the adults in my life, but I couldn't act that way with Leigh. My Emma-Bear.

That meant there was only one thing I *could* do.

I began making my way up the walk and finally found myself on the front porch. It took three tries before I could force myself to ring the doorbell. The doorbell chime sounded different. Or maybe I just didn't really remember what the chime sounded like at all. More than ten years ago, before the accident, I'd never bothered to ring the doorbell. I just knocked and then let myself in with the key Jo had given me.

No one answered. I went back down the three steps to

the walk, relieved and disappointed. Just then I heard the deadbolt flip. I turned around, but I didn't go up on the porch again.

"Curtis, hi," Leigh said, frowning as she pulled the door open. Her eyes had no tears now, but they looked red. The wind gusted by, and she folded her arms tight against her body. "Is something wrong?"

"You, uh...you weren't in school today."

"It was excused," Leigh said quickly. "My mom called the school this morning."

"No, I know," I said, holding out the envelope. "I wanted to bring—"

"Leigh, who is it?" a voice called from deeper in the house. "Honey, close the door," the voice went on, getting closer. "It's freezing..."

Jo came to the door wiping her hands on a towel, and she stopped short when she saw me. The blood drained from her face, and she dropped the towel. Her hands went to her mouth.

"Josh?" she said, her voice shaking.

I hadn't heard my given name in eight years; the name that Jo had insisted on giving to her son.

"Hi, Jo."

She came out the door and stood between Leigh and me. There was some gray in her dark hair, but it looked good on her. Her green eyes—the same exact shade of mine—had little red lines from crying earlier. I knew that if she smiled, a dimple would show up in her left cheek. I'd seen a mirror image of it in my own reflection countless times. When I smiled, that is.

"You cut your hair," I said. "I like it."

Leigh looked back and forth between us. "Josh? What—

Mom, this is Curtis, the guidance counselor who's subbing for Miz Peterson at school."

Jo put her arm around Leigh's shoulders. "Honey, this is my brother. Your Uncle Josh."

Leigh's eyes became big circles, and she turned back to me. "Your name isn't Curtis?"

I heaved a huge sigh and hung my head. "Curtis is my middle name. I started using it after I...after I moved away."

"You're...Uncle Josh?" Leigh asked.

I looked at her then, and I saw the little girl I'd loved so long ago.

"That's right, Emma-Bear. It's me."

The emotions on her face...I saw them all. Shock; disbelief; anger.

Then came the recognition.

Leigh let out a strangled sound, and she bolted back inside the house. A few seconds later, I heard a door slam and flinched. Jo came down the steps, and I moved back to make room for her on the walk.

"I'm sorry," she said, glancing at the door and then looking back at me. "It's just that today...well, it's a hard day for all of us."

I shook my head. "No, don't apologize. How...how are you?"

She scoffed. "Really? You come back after eight years, and that's all you can ask?"

I heard footsteps and then the voice I'd wanted to hear more than anyone's; it was also the voice I was afraid of hearing more than anyone else's.

My momma came toward the door.

"Joanna, sweetheart, what's going on? Who's at the—"

She came onto the porch. When we made eye contact, she put a hand to her chest. I shrugged.

"I'm home, Momma," I said, realizing in that moment just how right it felt to say those words. A smile started to cross my face, and I held open my arms. "I missed you."

She came down the steps in a flash and smacked me hard across the face. My skin began to burn, and I put a hand to my cheek.

"How dare you walk out on your family just when they needed you most? Do you have any idea what we've been through? Do you?"

Tears leaked from her eyes, and she threw her arms around me. The impact made me grunt and fall back half a step. I had a hard time breathing from how hard she squeezed.

"Don't you ever—*ever*, you hear me?—leave me like that again. You may be an adult, but I'm your mother, and I forbid it."

"I won't, Momma, I promise," I said, a hard lump pressing into my throat. "I'm so sorry I went away. I missed you so much. All of you. All I've wanted for the last eight years is to come home."

A minute later something knocked into me from the side, and I looked up to see Joanna squeezing us from my left. Footsteps thundered down the stairs, and then Leigh grabbed us from my right. She squeezed almost as hard as her grandmother did.

"Josh?"

I looked around the women and saw Kirk standing in the doorway.

"Hey, buddy," I said. "I, uh...decided to come home."

Kirk grinned at me, and he joined the group. We all

stood there holding each other for a while, not saying anything, but I was willing to bet everyone else was thinking the same thing I was: that for the first time in a long time, Christmas would be exactly as it was meant to be.

Mr. C. stared at the computer, a little skeptical and in awe all at the same time.

"I still can't believe I can actually see you and talk to you in real time," he said to the screen.

"That's what I keep telling you, sir. It'll make it so much easier for you to keep in touch with everyone you've got on the ground."

"Speaking of which, you're sure Curtis doesn't want to come back?" Mr. C. said, peering over his glasses.

"I'm sure, sir. He said he might actually want to go back to school after all. He's not sure what he wants to do next, but he knows he wants to stay with his family."

Mr. C. sat back in his chair and folded his hands over his stomach. His wife had nagged him to start exercising again, and he thought he just might actually get into it once they all got through the Night Of run this year. But he also knew part of his problem was that he was just getting too old for all of this excitement.

"It's a shame," he said. "I was hoping to get him to fly as my co-pilot on the Night Of. Maybe even start training him to become the lead pilot."

"Why, sir? Are you all right?"

"Oh, nothing's wrong with me," Mr. C. said, waving the possibility away. "Doesn't hurt to be prepared, though. In any case, I am happy that things worked out the way they were supposed to. It's about time, right? I guess I'll have to start working on his Reintegration paperwork."

There was a pause, and Mr. C. couldn't resist peeking

at the little square in the corner of the screen that showed his own face. Remarkable, what technology could let him do these days.

"Sir, could I ask you a question?"

Mr. C. sat up and started moving some papers around on his desk. "Certainly."

"How did you know? What if Curtis had really shut down the whole idea of going back to his family?"

Mr. C. grinned. He couldn't remember the number of times his elves had expressed wonderment about how he knew something would happen. These young whipper-snappers didn't realize he'd been around for a long time. Times changed—fashions changed, he noted wryly, as he glanced down at his jeans—but people didn't. And the longer he lived, the more life experience he had to help them.

He shrugged. "Just a hunch. Now get off the blasted computer so I can do some work. I've still got a Night Of run to plan."

"Yes, sir. I'll be in touch soon."

December 20, 2015
New Horizons Prep Academy
Salt Lake City, Utah

Prerna shut down her laptop and put it in her bag before anyone could see who she was talking to. School only had about two hours to go before winter break started, and the chances were slim that any of the students would need help. Still, it didn't hurt to be cautious.

She heaved a sigh of relief as she turned to her desktop computer. Curtis, the last elf on her list, had finally come home. She'd started wondering just how long she would have to stick it out here in Salt Lake to help all the elves who were in this Assignment.

The Rockies had dominated her vision as she drove to and from her townhome for the last six years. She found them beautiful, formidable, and the source of all the cold weather she detested. Mr. C. had promised that the minute Curtis reunited with his family, she could apply for a position in a warmer climate.

With Christmas carols playing softly in the background, Prerna began googling secretarial jobs and available apartments in Rio.

Acknowledgments

I've written many stories over my lifetime. Hundreds. Some I wrote as part of the writing workshop I designed for myself back when I couldn't afford to attend workshops with other writers and real instructors. Others I wrote because of writing prompts that intrigued me or for contests.

A lot of those stories were about getting words on the page, about sticking to a regular writing practice of posting new work. Sort of like brushing your teeth— necessary for good health but not exactly the most enthralling activity. Some made me grin with the discoveries I made about new characters and the possibilities of new plots.

Then there are stories like this one.

This novella started as a writing exercise to force me out of my comfort zone. (For the writers who are curious, I'm a plotter by nature. I decided to try to pants my way through something new.) That particular writing exercise didn't get me very far, but the core of the story—about an elf who is afraid to fly and yet is somehow key to Santa's annual trip around the world—that stuck with me.

I started doing research on flying and planes and accidents, and Curtis's voice fell into my brain. It came through fully formed. I wasn't so much writing a novella as I was recording what he told me.

I submitted this story to many different publications and contests. Lots of rejections. I forced myself to put it to the side for a while so I could work on other things. I even thought that maybe this book wouldn't ever get past my hard drive. But Curtis's story wouldn't let me go. I knew I had to find a way to share it with the world, and I'm deeply honored and grateful that now I get to do so.

Of course, I didn't do this on my own. I couldn't. Writing is a solitary pursuit, but publishing is a team sport all the way. That team helped this dream of mine come true. Any success that comes from this book belongs as much to you as me.

Jennie: my alpha reader, my first editor on all important writing things I do, and my writing soulmate. Thank you for helping me shape Curtis's story all those years ago. I would never have gotten this far without your willingness to indulge what started out sounding like a wacky idea.

To the entire team at Atmosphere Press: you've all been exceptional, and I'm still in awe of the fact that you made my first book-length publication a reality. I feel like I've found my publishing home, and I don't want to move out!

Nick, thank you for taking a chance on *Elves* in the first place.

Asata, my Atmosphere editor, your insight and thoughtful questions elevated the story. Prerna wouldn't have become an elf if it hadn't been for you.

Ronaldo, thank you for guiding the conversation when it came to the cover design and your patience with sending all my requests to Kevin.

Kevin, you made my mother cry with the cover you designed—thank you so much! Every author dreams of seeing those happy tears from her mom. You managed to capture the beauty and melancholy of Curtis's world in a way that has imprinted itself onto my heart. Your stunning cover will always be my favorite of anything I ever do, because it was the first.

Kathi, Bette, Cari, thank you for being sounding boards on cover options. All of you are dear, precious writing and publishing friends, and I count myself richer for knowing you.

To my family, of course, for putting up with my writerly self. Your support is everything.

And to you, dear readers. During my first conversation with her, Asata mentioned that some of you might find solace in this story because grief and loss are very real experiences during the holidays. I hope you do find it helpful. I write as much to understand things as to share them. I hope you get some measure of both in this story.

All my love,
E. :>

Author's Note

If you enjoyed this book, please take a minute to leave a review on your favorite online outlets. It can be just a sentence or two, but that support is crucial in helping indie authors to keep writing. Please feel free to reach out and let me know what you thought of this story. Thank you, so much, in advance.

About Atmosphere Press

Atmosphere Press is an independent, full-service publisher for excellent books in all genres and for all audiences. Learn more about what we do at atmospherepress.com.

We encourage you to check out some of Atmosphere's latest releases, which are available at Amazon.com and via order from your local bookstore:

The Embers of Tradition, a novel by Chukwudum Okeke

Saints and Martyrs: A Novel, by Aaron Roe

When I Am Ashes, a novel by Amber Rose

Melancholy Vision: A Revolution Series Novel, by L.C. Hamilton

The Recoleta Stories, by Bryon Esmond Butler

Voodoo Hideaway, a novel by Vance Cariaga

Hart Street and Main, a novel by Tabitha Sprunger

The Weed Lady, a novel by Shea R. Embry

A Book of Life, a novel by David Ellis

It Was Called a Home, a novel by Brian Nisun

Grace, a novel by Nancy Allen

Shifted, a novel by KristaLyn A. Vetovich

Because the Sky is a Thousand Soft Hurts, stories by Elizabeth Kirschner

About the Author:

Since starting in publishing in 2005, Ekta has written and edited about everything from healthcare to home improvement to Hindi films. She became a freelance editor in 2011 and believes words have the power to change people and the world. A writing contest judge and magazine editor, Ekta also hosts Biblio Breakdown where she talks about the craft and offers writing exercises (https://ektargarg.com/biblio-breakdown-the-writing-podcast/).

Ekta reads at least one book a week (which will definitely go up when the kids go to college.) She also manages The Write Edge (http://thewriteedge.wordpress.com) where writers can connect with her for editing help and where she showcases her original fiction, book reviews, and parenting adventures. When she's not working on stories, Ekta spends time with friends, keeps up with the latest Bollywood gossip, and dances in the kitchen while she's making dinner. She lives in Central Illinois with her husband and family. *The Truth About Elves* is her first book.

Made in the USA
Monee, IL
04 October 2022

15066723R00080